SHERLOCK HOLMES
and the
ARABIAN PRINCESS

SHERLOCK HOLMES and the ARABIAN PRINCESS

John North

IAN HENRY PUBLICATIONS

Based on the musical play
"Sherlock Holmes in the Deerstalker"
by Terence Mustoo
music & lyrics by Doug Flack
© copyright, Terence Mustoo, 1984
© copyright, Douglas Flack, 1984

This novelisation, © copyright I H Wilkes, 1990

ISBN 0 86025 270 1

Printed by
Biddles Ltd.
Guildford & King's Lynn
for
Ian Henry Publications, Ltd.
20 Park Drive, Romford, Essex RM1 4LH

INTRODUCTION

INTRODUCTION

My previous story about Sherlock Holmes with a theatrical background* has been very well received and I have been encouraged to retrieve from my files a further exploit of the great detective. I had been dissuaded from publishing this piece by my dear wife, who claimed that it showed her up in a less than favourable light. While I bowed to her wishes at the time, as a widower for a second time I have, on re-reading the manuscript, found little cause for embarrassment.

Sherlock Holmes himself, in retirement in Sussex, has treated the episode in his usual off-hand fashion. I did, however, notice on his mantlepiece in his small cottage two picture frames with ladies' portraits therein. One was of Irene Adler, a protagonist from the spring of 1889, while the other was of Lily Nightingale, a music hall artiste who you will meet in the following pages.

JOHN H WATSON, MD
Southsea
November, 1928

*Sherlock Holmes and the Eminent Thespian

3

THE DISAPPEARANCE

THE DISAPPEARANCE

In the spring of the year 1902 I had been inspecting a possible consulting room in Queen Anne Street. I had been out of practice for some time, although I flatter myself that the name John H Watson had not been forgotten in the field of tropical medicine. As a widower in comfortable circumstances I had whiled away my time assisting my friend, Sherlock Holmes, in a few of his investigations – then to annoy him somewhat by recording my recollections of these cases and having them published in the *Strand* magazine. My friend regarded my literary endeavours with scepticism, but I only ever published with his express permission and I justified my work by arguing that the world should be able to share my appreciation of his keen brain and deductive reasoning.

I have to admit that these trivia, as Holmes called them, had paid handsomely in royalties and that by this time I had become an established author, enjoying particular success with *The Hound of the Baskervilles*, which had been published in book form early that year, having already had a *succès d'éstime* in the *Strand* the previous autumn.

We had been on Dartmoor with the unfortunate Baskerville family in September, 1900, and since then I had only joined my friend in a single investigation, that concerning Mr Neil Gibson, the Gold King. I felt that Holmes and I were growing apart: his time was increasingly occupied with pure research into forensic studies, while I was either scribble, scribble, scribble or travelling in my beloved Scotland.

I had spent the Easter holiday with friends in Angus and journeyed home to London by way of Edinburgh, where I fell in with some old medical friends. They had chaffed me about my idleness and, when I got back to London, I determined to resume my practice.

Thus, I was in Queen Anne Street, having looked over a promising set of chambers, when I became aware of the newsboy on the corner of Welbeck Street hawking his wares by crying, "Disappearance of Princess! Music Hall mystery!" I was sufficiently intrigued to purchase a copy of the *Evening Standard* and, having perused the main story, felt that I should visit 221b Baker Street forthwith.

I was let into the old rooms by the ageless Mrs Hudson and found Holmes engrossed with his test tubes and a newly opened parcel. "Sit down a minute, old friend," he said without other greeting, "I have just received a parcel from an American acquaintance enclosing samples of American tobacco ash and I am bound to check them against my collection: so far he hasn't beaten me, but there are still twenty-three samples to be checked."

As he busied himself I was able to more thoroughly read the newspaper, so that, when he finally turned towards me, I was in possession of all the facts that the reporter had seen fit to print.

"Johnson had me foxed on just one sample. But then I read from the label on the packet that it is a newly introduced strain, so perhaps my old fashioned methods are not so bad after all."

"Have you seen the news, Holmes?" I enquired.

"Upon what subject? The South African Peace Conference, for example?"

"No, nearer home than that, Holmes," and I proffered the evening paper with its bold headline about the disappeared princess.

Quickly Holmes read through the article and then said, "Intriguing, but I am sure that Scotland Yard have the matter in hand. I was never one, as you know, for offering unsolicited advice."

"But don't you see, Holmes, that the police have a clue?"

"Certainly, but that makes my participation even less essential, I should have thought."

"At the scene of the disappearance the police have found a deerstalker hat and they say that two of the chorus girls report seeing a tall, thin man in a cape-backed Donegal running away from the backstage area."

"I did read that," agreed Holmes.

"You must see that that description fits you exactly."

"Along with a thousand other people in London. You surely don't think, do you, Watson, that I had anything to do with this girl's vanishing trick?"

I rose from my chair and paced restlessly around the room, "Of course not, Holmes, but what I think isn't important. Sooner or later someone in the yellow press is going to observe that the great Sherlock Holmes fits the known description and, unless the matter is cleared up satisfactorily, there will be a lurking suspicion left in the public mind that you are involved in some way. It could do untold harm for your reputation."

9

Holmes flushed, "If you are suggesting, Watson, that my standing is sufficiently slight to be damaged by the gutter press and such a preposterous story I have to say that it must be a very evanescent reputation."

My perambulation of the room had taken me to the window. Looking down I espied a figure passing by on the opposite side of Baker Street. I called Holmes to my side and pointed to the man, saying, "Now, I shall demonstrate how much of your methods I have assimilated over the years. I can tell you that man is in trade, works in a small shop without much light, handles chalk and does very fine work, although he has a marked lack of imagination."

I had the pleasure of seeing Sherlock Holmes for once almost bereft of speech. After giving me a very strange look he asked, "May I be told how you deduce all that from this distance?"

"Certainly. He is my tailor," I admitted.

It had been a long time since I had seen Holmes so annoyed. "You are making a mockery of my system of observation," he almost growled. "I can tell, for instance, that you have been for a walk in Hyde Park this morning, that you then visited premises in your search for rooms and that you then purchased a newspaper."

I was amazed. "How can you tell all that, Holmes," I enquired.

"Simple. There are newly made scuff marks on your boots, showing that you recently cleaned them on a scraper. As the only place where you might have picked mud up on your boots this morning would have been in a public park, as I know you like feeding the ducks and as Hyde Park is the nearest open space with mud and ducks, I think it a fair assumption that you have been in Hyde Park, probably down by the Serpentine. I also know that you are looking for chambers and I see on your left sleeve house dust, presumably picked up by contact with an unclean surface in an empty room."

"But what about the newspaper?" I asked.

Holmes, his good humour restored by his simple demonstration, gave me a tight smile, "You brought it into these rooms and showed it to me, didn't you?"

That is the trouble with Holmes, his thought processes are so fast that very often my own mind just stops.

Holmes started filling his calabash with shag. This is one of his habits that I have had occasion to complain about over the years, but it is, I suppose, less pernicious than his heroin addiction, so I have to put up with the foul smoke that he claims helps his thought processes.

"It might be a useful mental exercise," he mused, "to examine this disappearance a little more closely. Not, you understand, that I intend to interfere in any way, but if the problem can be solved simply by sitting here and thinking the ramifications through, I might then explain it all to Lestrade by the telephone. Now then, recapitulate the events of last night as you have understood them."

"Well," I started, "this Arabian princess Fatima – is on a private visit to London and she insisted, being a very imperious young lady, that she see a performance at a London music hall. The authorities were consulted and selected the Hyperion in the Strand, as being the theatre they could best police. The princess, her bodyguard and her guardian in London went by cab from her hotel in Bloomsbury to the music hall. They had got about half way through the first half of the performance when a magician, now, what was his name..." and I searched through the newspaper columns, "... ah, yes, The

11

Great Marvo, asked for a member of the audience to come on stage to assist in a disappearing lady trick. Before any of her entourage could stop her this young madam jumps up and volunteers. Then, on stage, in front of a packed audience, Mister Marvo drapes a cloth over the princess, mutters a bit of hocus-pocus, waves his wand and the young lady disappears. And then stays disappeared!"

"Where were the police during all this time, do you suppose," queried Holmes.

"According to the newspaper they were all fixed in their stall seats uncertain of what to do, but certain that Marvo's trick was simply the usual music hall deception. He's 'helping the police with their enquiries', according to this."

"How many police were present?"

"It doesn't say, but Inspector George Lestrade was in charge."

"Poor old Lestrade. He can't be far off honourable retirement. And now this. Oh, dear," Holmes smiled, "but it isn't very funny."

"Can you see any obvious solution?" I asked.

Holmes was about to reply when we heard the front door bell ring and Mrs Hudson scurry along the downstairs corridor to answer it. There was a few seconds muttered conversation and then steps began to come upstairs.

"Come along, now, Watson," said my friend, "use your recently demonstrated deductive skills to tell me who we can expect."

"Well," I said slowly, "it is a slow, but rather timorous tread of someone not used to large houses, possibly wearing hobnail boots, but lacking inner confidence. It could well be Joe, the bootblack boy."

"Good try, Watson, but it's..."

"The Reverend Charles Samuels," announced Mrs Hudson.

Our visitor came into the room. Dressed in

12

black and holding his clerical hat in hand, I could not see his parson's dog collar underneath a substantial beard that almost submerged the lower part of his face. His light blue eyes gave the appearance of peering through dark brown undergrowth as his hair style also tended to the exuberant.

Mrs Hudson, giving our visitor a look that seemed to say that she preferred men of the cloth to be clean shaven, said that she was baking cakes downstairs and would come if wanted and departed.

"Ah, Mr Holmes," said Mr Samuels, shaking me warmly by the hand.

I indicated that I was not the detective and, after the confusion had been resolved, Holmes sat Mr Samuels in a chair - my chair - and asked how he could help.

"I have come to you for help," said Mr Samuels. "You may have seen about the disappearance of the Princess Fatima. I am her guardian in London."

"We were just discussing the matter as you arrived, Mr Samuels, please accept our sympathy in your embarrassing loss."

I interposed, "If you don't mind my asking, why were you made her guardian in this country?"

"It is a long story, going back over many years. King Aziz and I met when I was an Anglican missionary in Arabia. One night, while I was staying in his camp I had occasion to return to his tent during the night to return one of his books. As I pushed up the tent flap I saw a snake just about to strike the sleeping King. I smashed it over the head with the Bible and so saved the King's life. Since then we've been close friends."

"That shows the power of the Good Book to the heathens, right enough," said Holmes and I looked at him sharply as he does not usually indulge

13

in facetiousness.

To change the subject I interjected, "That reminds me of an experience I once had in Afghanistan, when a yak..."

Holmes rudely cut into my reminiscence, saying, "Surely, the King would have provided a bodyguard as well as yourself. The Mohammedans are very strict about the liberties they allow their unmarried females."

"Certainly, we usually had the services of Ben Achmed, but he was unwell. I think he had been drinking the water. But I felt secure from harm as we had a police presence at the music hall amounting to some eight constables and an inspector. And I regarded the presence of an audience to be a guarantee of safety in itself. Nobody, outside our immediate circle and the police, had known we were going to the Hyperion, so no danger to the princess could have been arranged in advance."

Holmes pondered for a few seconds. "That suggests that either there is a spy in your own party or someone in Scotland Yard passed the information on to outsiders. Tell me, why do you think the princess has been kidnapped."

"But we don't know that she has been kidnapped, Mr Holmes," replied the hirsute clergyman, "she has simply disappeared!"

"Nevertheless," pursued Holmes, "I think it unlikely that a stage magician, however gifted, could cause a real disappearance. We must work on the presumption that Princess Fatima has been abducted for felonious purposes."

"I cannot believe that Fatima has been taken for gain. Her father, although wealthy by Arabian standards, is little more than a nomadic tribesman. The territory of Kuwait, where he resides, is a very poor country, even though it has been a British

14

Protectorate for the past three years. It is because of the British connection that King Aziz sent his only daughter - for he is almost celibate by Arabian standards - to England. He wanted her to bring back to him some British culture so that he could treat with the British Chargé d'Affaires more as an equal."

It is one of the perennial delights of knowing Sherlock Holmes that he can sometimes amaze one with his knowledge of obscure subjects and I was surprised to now learn that he had a smattering, at least, of the geology of the Persian Gulf.

"Kuwait may be a poor desert country now, Mr Samuels, but I have felt for some time that there should be some exploration made in that area. I have heard reports of crude oil ponds in the sands in that region. With the coming dominance that I forsee of the internal combustion engine your nomadic King could turn into a world financial power."

I felt that the conversation was straying from the matter in hand. "But what about the Princess?" I prompted.

"Yes. Perhaps, Mr Samuels, you could tell us exactly what happened in the music hall last night."

"Of course. We arrived in good time for the eight thirty performance and took our seats in the third row of the stalls."

"Where in the row were the seats, Mr Samuels?" asked Holmes.

"Because we were late in booking - I had gone to the music hall advance booking office myself early yesterday afternoon - we had three seats right at the end of the row and I sat in Seat Thirty-One and the police inspector, whose name I did not quite catch -"

"Lestrade," I interjected.

"- the police inspector," continued the reverend gentleman, "in Seat Twenty-Nine, with

Fatima between us. I have to say that I had not been to this form of entertainment before, so everything was novel to me. On the side of the stage there was a gentleman who was referred to as the Chairman, who was wearing rather flamboyant evening dress. His waistcoat was like Joseph's coat of many colours. His function was to introduce the various acts and to jolly the audience along if they got restive. You will understand that a lot has happened since then and my memory of the earlier performers is rather jumbled, but the curtain first went up on a chorus line of about eight girls who sang a rather naughty song about railway porters and what they did in their spare time. I don't think Fatima understood or I would have insisted we leave then."

"Most of the material of the modern music hall," said Holmes, "is more risqué in the content than in the meaning."

"Quite so. Then there was a rather well-built lady who sang an aria: her voice had seen better days, I fear. And she was followed by a gentleman who did very strange contortions on a bicycle. I can't remember either of their names, I am afraid."

"If they are significant, I am sure that we can establish who they were," said Holmes.

"Then there was a tenor called Shamus O'Flynn - I think he might have been Irish - who sang a song about his mother. This wasn't very well received by the audience and I can't say I blamed them. He just hadn't got a very good voice and the audience cat-called a little. And then there was another act. What was it?" Mr Samuels paused to search his mind. "No, I can't remember at all. And then the Chairman announced The Great Marvo, who he said had baffled all the Crowned Heads of Europe with his magic."

"One minute, please," said Holmes, "I might have record of him in my indexes." And he crossed to his filing cabinets and riffled through his extensive cuttings and other memorabilia. "Ah, yes," he said with pleasure in his voice, "here we are. The Great Marvo. His real name is Fred Marlow and he made his first appearance as a magician at Wilton's Music Hall on the eighteenth of June, 1877. Since then he has played the music halls around the country, but I have no record of any continental tours, although I am bound to say that my indexes are not quite as exhaustive on the other side of the Channel as I would wish. However, pray continue, Mr Samuels."

Mr Samuels seemed taken aback by this demonstration of my friend's comprehensive knowledge of such an obscure music hall artist and, I must admit, I was similarly impressed, even though Holmes had demonstrated this aspect of his forensic skill on many previous occasions.

"Yes, well," Mr Samuels hesitated. "Perhaps you can tell me more about the performance than I thought I saw, Mr Holmes?"

"No, no, pray continue. I am afraid that I was showing off slightly. I do not keep records of all the minor artists who appear on the boards, but I do try to keep a file on all presdigitators and conjurers: one never knows when light-fingered gentry of that art might not turn to crime to supplement what can be a meagre living on the stage."

The reverend gentleman took up the threads of his narrative again. "Well, Marvo used two of the girls who I think were in the chorus as assistants in his act and, with their help, he produced the flags of all nations and flowers from a top hat and then he did some very clever manipulation of some playing cards. Next he asked for a male volunteer from the audience and a gentleman with white flowing locks stood up from a seat immediately in front of us and went on stage. I think he might have been a friend of Marvo's because he stood without

17

any hesitation in front of a board into which Marvo threw some very deadly looking knives. And then Marvo asked if a lady in the audience would come on stage, please. Immediately Fatima jumped up. I argued with her as I was afraid that she might be putting herself at risk from another knife-throwing exhibition, but she is a very head-strong young lady and she pushed past me and ran on to the stage by the steps that lead up from the stalls."

"Didn't the police inspector try to stop her running off like that?" asked Holmes.

"He didn't move a muscle," averred Mr Samuels. "When she got on stage Marvo announced that he was now going to make this young lady disappear. Then he said jocularly in my direction that her friends weren't to worry as she would come back in an unexpected way. He positioned her carefully on the stage and, although I was anxious, I assumed that he was putting her over one of the trap doors to the understage and that she would be met down there by one of Marvo's minions and brought back to stage level in a few minutes. Well, when he had stood her where he wanted her, he said for her to stand perfectly still and then he threw a black silk cape over her."

"Did this cape reach the floor?" queried Holmes.

"Oh, yes, easily. Fatima is barely five feet tall, so there was ample cape to cover all of her. When she was covered Marvo made a few magic passes around the front of the cloaked figure and then - pouf - he set fire to some sort of firework on the dummy where he had put one of Fatima's necklaces, which went off with a bang. When we in the audience re-opened our eyes, the cloak was lying in a little heap in the middle of the stage. Naturally, we all applauded and Marvo whisked the cloak away to show that there was nothing there.

He then made no reference to the disappearance and went on with another trick that involved producing little balls of fluff into his hands - down his sleeves, I should imagine."

"Wait a minute," said Holmes, "can you tell me exactly who was on stage at the time of the vanishing trick?"

Mr Samuels thought for a second. "Yes, of course. There was Marvo, obviously, and then there were the two chorus girls - they had helped Marvo drape the cloth over Fatima and then held it at about her head height until the thunderflash thing. And the white headed man from the audience was still there somewhere. And I think that the Chairman was sitting at his table right in the far corner."

"Did the white headed man return to the audience after the show?"

"I regret I did not notice, because, after the fluff ball trick, Marvo said words to the effect 'Oh, I forgot, perhaps we should return the young lady to her friends' and he made some cabalistic passes towards the back of the stage and then made a big flourishing gesture - and nothing happened! Marvo laughed and said that perhaps the spirits of the theatre who would return the young lady had not heard the drum roll, but that 'Here she was' and again nothing happened. At that the Inspector jumped up out of his seat and dashed on stage. I thought he was being a little embarrassing - "

"Lestrade all over," I muttered.

"- and he demanded that the show stop until Fatima was returned safe and sound. Naturally the audience wasn't very pleased and shouted and booed at him, but - what d'you call him? - Lestrade called his police from the back of the hall where they had been standing, watching the performance, and the audience realised that something was genuinely

19

wrong. Being British they rallied round and the audience looked under seats and so on and in the public parts of the theatre, while the inspector and his men and the theatre staff searched the rest of the hall. Meanwhile the music hall orchestra played popular numbers and, eventually, everyone had to admit that Fatima (although no one told the audience who she was) had simply vanished into thin air."

"What were you doing all this time, Mr Samuels," asked Holmes.

"I wandered round behind the scenes backstage, they call it in the theatre – and peered into a few dressing rooms. Very confusing it all was. At one stage I wandered into the chorus girls' room and modesty forbids that I repeat what I saw."

"And what was Marvo doing?"

"I don't know. He went into the wings with a policeman when Lestrade took over and I didn't see him again."

Holmes put his fingers together and gazed at the ceiling for a few moments. "How long did it take for Lestrade and yourself to establish that Fatima was no longer in the theatre?"

"After about twenty-five minutes we felt the case was hopeless and so Lestrade permitted the performance to continue. By then more police had arrived and they were posted all round the building, inside and out. At the end of the performance I understand that everyone leaving was scrutinised most carefully, but Fatima was gone. I had left before then, I was far too upset to stay and watch people enjoying themselves."

"Did you go straight back to your hotel, Mr Samuels?"

"Of course. We have been staying in a suite in the Excalibur Hotel for the past three weeks and last night I went to my room to pass a sleepless

20

night. The inspector came round this morning to report that there was no progress, but that he had been forced to tell the press about the matter. There were so many people in the audience that it could hardly be kept a secret. I sat in my hotel room, hoping against hope that Fatima would just come back to me, but then I made up my mind to come to see you to implore you to help me. I could never face King Aziz again if the girl came to any harm while in my guardianship."

"But you have read the newspaper reports about the case, haven't you?" asked Holmes. "Didn't you see that the police had gathered some clues?"

"To be honest with you, Mr Holmes," said the clergyman, "it was those clues that brought you to mind."

I flashed a look at Holmes, to indicate 'I told you so.'

"I have heard of your prowess through Doctor Watson's admirably written stories -"

I bowed my head to the compliment, but Holmes didn't look too pleased - he can be very jealous sometimes.

"- and felt that you must be able to assist me in my plight."

"The best thing we can do," I offered, "is to pray that the princess will materialise again somewhere accessible."

"Perhaps you will leave the praying to me," retorted Samuels, somewhat acidly I felt. "I had hoped that Mr Holmes might be able to make some rather more tangible moves to restore the princess to me."

"If anyone can help you, Holmes can," I said, rather stiffly, for I felt that Mr Samuels had dealt rather harshly with my comment, which had been meant to lighten the atmosphere.

"Thank you for your confidence, Watson. I shall

21

certainly be pleased to look into your riddle, Mr Samuels."

"Money is no object," said the clergyman, "just get my little lady back safe to me."

"We'll see about that all in good time," replied Holmes. "And now, if you will excuse me, Mr Samuels, I will start my investigation forthwith."

"Excuse me," I interjected, "have you a picture of the princess?"

"I doubt that very much," said Holmes, "people from the Persian area do not normally allow themselves to be represented pictorially. But I must agree that a verbal description might be useful."

"Certainly, Mr Holmes. She is a very slight girl aged only seventeen. Later, perhaps, she may take after her mother and run to fat, but presently she is a mere slip of a thing. She has black hair and dark brown eyes, with what I detect as a gold fleck in them. Possibly the most distinctive thing about her - when I last saw her, of course - was that she was wearing what are popularly known as harem pants, in gold with green netting over them, and a matching covering to her, er, chest: she had gold slippers on, as well. Oh, and a net veil over her face."

"Isn't that a trifle exotic for the English climate, Mr Samuels?" asked Holmes.

"Oh, I agree," said the clergyman, "normally in this country she has been wearing rather less noticeable clothes, but she insisted that she put on her normal dress for this particular outing and when a princess insists..." and Mr Samuels spread his hands in a gesture denoting his lack of influence over his obviously headstrong young charge.

"Thank you, Mr Samuels," said Holmes, "well, if we are going to find the Princess Fatima, we had better start straight away. So, if you will excuse me?"

"Oh, of course," and Mr Samuels rose to his feet. "I'll show myself out, shall I?"

Holmes can be very offhand occasionally and simply waved a limp hand towards the door in farewell. However, I am one of the old school and saw the ex-missionary to the door and raised a farewell hand to him as he descended the stairs to the front door.

When I returned to the room Holmes was again buried in his filing system. "Samuels, Samuels," he was saying under his breath.

"What is it, old fellow?" I asked.

"I have no record of a Charles Samuels in my files," said my friend, "but I cannot expect to find details of every subject of the King there, I suppose."

"Shall I send Joe out for the other evening papers?" I am not unaware of how an investigation should begin.

"No. First we'll go to the music hall."

"That sounds jolly," I said.

Holmes, whose sense of humour is sadly lacking on occasion, said, "We are going to work, not play, Watson." And he grabbed his outdoor clothes and strode out. I followed, shouting in the downstairs corridor to Mrs Hudson, to tell her that we were once more employed on a case.

THE MUSIC HALL

THE MUSIC HALL

The Hyperion is one of our newer music halls and, like the Savoy Theatre a few yards further down the Strand, has all the most modern devices, including electric light. The foyer is delightfully rococo, being decorated with cherubim and nymphs, all sporting away in their gilt finery. The marble floor was inlaid with representations of nine young ladies, who I imagine were meant to be the Muses. One could see why the highest priced stall seats cost ten shillings: an exhorbitant price, but clearly this was a superior type of music hall, not one of the old spit and sawdust variety theatres that still abounded in the provincial cities or in the eastern suburbs of our capital.

Entering the auditorium as we did after having exchanged a few explanatory words with the commissionaire resplendent in what looked like an Indian Maharajah's outfit, again the red plush velvet and the decorations on the balcony façades and above the stage demonstrated clearly that this was a superior place of entertainment.

However, one's eye did not immediately take all this in, as there was some sort of rehearsal taking place on stage as we entered the back of the auditorium.

In the middle of the stage was a large gentleman in shirtsleeves and braces, perspiring freely as he tried to control both the girls prancing in front of him and the orchestra in the pit behind him. We watched silently for some time, during which the producer - for so I assumed him to be - got some sort of order out of chaos. After about ten minutes the lead singer and her backing chorus finished their song more or less simultaneously with the pit orchestra: it had been a difficult number to 'put over' (as they say in the theatre) and the performance prompted me to applaud loudly.

The producer swung round and peered into the darkness of the auditorium. "'Ere, who's there? You didn't ought to be in 'ere. Git art!"

Holmes strolled down the centre gangway and then across the front of Row A to the left of the stage and climbed the steps leading on to the stage.

"My name is Sherlock Holmes," he introduced himself, "and this is my companion, Doctor John Watson."

"I don't care if you are King Solomon and your mate is the Queen of Sheba, chummy," said the producer, who, now we were close to him, seemed a very large and menacing figure, "nobody don't come into the featre while we're rehearsin', see?"

"Would you let me in were I an Arabian Princess?" asked Holmes.

"Nah, look 'ere, I don't..."

"I have been requested to investigate the disappearance that took place here last night."

"Not another one. Look, I've been knee deep in rozzers ever since it happened. If I've told one I don't know nuffin' about it, I've told half a dozen - and so have all me staff - and these girls. And Marvo's still dahn at the nick making a statement. So don't bovver me any more. I've got a livin' to earn and I've got these dozy dinahs to sing a new song proper before tonight's shows. Nah - git." And the producer rolled up the right sleeve of his rather grubby shirt, revealing a tattoo of crossed hearts and the words 'Alf' and 'Gertie'.

As 'Alf' advanced towards us, the principal chorine intervened, "Don't be so hasty, Alf, I'm sure this gentleman -" and she fluttered her eyelashes at Holmes, rather forwardly, I thought - "is only here to help. Leave this to me."

She pushed Alf back and stepped forward herself. "Are you really Sherlock Holmes, the famous detective? I've read all those fascinating stories about you."

"I am Sherlock Holmes, madam," said he, somewhat stiff lipped.

"My name's Lily Nightingale," said the young lady, who, when I came to look rather more closely at her, might not have been quite so young as her initial appearance might have led one to believe, "and this is Alf Barker. He's our producer and he's the Chairman of the Music Hall, as well."

"Im delighted to make your acquaintance, Miss Nightingale. And yours, Mr Barker."

"Oh, yes, and these are Tilly, Rose, Beth, Pearl, Ivy, Marie and Lottie. The Hyperion girls."

The girls simpered at us and one of them sidled over to me. "Are you really Doctor Watson, the great author?"

I had to admit the charge and I was then enormously embarrassed that she slid her arm into mine and more or less clung on to me while Holmes and Miss Nightingale continued their conversation.

"Of course, we all want to help, don't we, girls?" And the girls all bobbed and nodded.

"Oh, all right," growled Barker, "but for Gaud's sake, don't take too long about it. We've got an extra matinée today and I've got to get on."

"Why have you an extra performance?" enquired Holmes.

"Public demand," explained Barker.

"Sensation seekers, I'd call 'em," said one of the girls, who unfortunately suffered from a slight lisp.

"So this disappearance business has actually increased your business?"

"Now look 'ere," bristled Barker, "I don't need no kidnappin' to improve my takin's. And, anyway, there'll be a riot if Marvo ain't back from the cops in time to do his bit. That's what they all want to see, you see."

Another of the girls giggled, "Anything for publicity, that's our Alf."

I thought Barker was going to strike her, but a couple of other girls stepped in front of Barker as he crossed menacingly to the girl who had cheeked him.

He contented himself by saying, "That's not funny, Pearl."

She bridled a bit and muttered, "Pardon me for breathing, I'm sure." And then she surprised me by pushing between her two companions and going over to Barker and, standing on tip-toe, giving him a kiss on his forehead.

I suppose these theatre people have a different moral code to the rest of us, but I did think this a trifle forward, especially in mixed company. To divert attention from what I regarded as an intimate incident, I said, "Please, ladies, we do have some questions and the quicker we get them answered, the quicker you will be able to get back to your dancing and singing."

The young person who had hold of my arm, squeezed it and said, "Of course you do - and you have such a masterful way with you. By the way, my name's Tilly Footage."

30

I coloured slightly and tried to put things on a more formal basis. "How d'you do, my dear?"

"Lovely - since I saw you, Doctor dear," said the young lady, who seemed to me to be a big girl for dancing. I put my bowler hat on the Chairman's table and mopped my brow with my handkerchief: I don't think I had been in such close proximity to a female person since my wife had passed on.

Holmes took command of the situation. "May we continue?" he asked in an exasperated tone of voice.

Miss Nightingale said, "Of course, what do you want to know?"

"First, where were all you young ladies when the disappearance took place?"

"We were all in our dressing room changing for the next number and we didn't know anything about it until later."

"And you, Mr Barker?"

"As it 'appens, I slipped off backstage during Marvo's act - to get meself a glass of water," said the Chairman.

The girl who had unexpectedly kissed him, said, "Glass of gin, more like!" And she received a slap on her posterior for her pains.

"According to my informants, some of you chorus girls were assisting Marvo in his act."

"Oh, yes, of course," admitted Miss Nightingale. "Last night it was you four, wasn't it?"

Some of the girls seeped forward, reluctantly, I felt.

The one who had identified herself as Pearl said, "Me and Lottie was on stage holding the cloak over the girl, but we was both looking out into the audience and giving them a bit of the old you-know-what."

"I beg you pardon," I said, almost involuntarily.

"Go on," said Tilly, "you know, you great big

31

lovely man, you."

I didn't feel inclined to pursue this particular point in these circumstances, mainly because the young female was pressing certain portions of her anatomy rather closer to mine than I thought decorous.

"So you didn't see anything?" asked Holmes.

"Not a whisker," Lottie spoke for the first time.

"And what about you two?" Holmes turned to the other young persons who had stepped forward.

"We were both under the stage when the trick was being done, so as we could collect the audience member when she dropped down on the trap and then bring her back up again to stage level to make her reappearance."

"I see, Miss - er..."

"Oh, I'm Beth Sessions," it was, of course, the girl who lisped, "and this is Rose Pitman."

"And what happened beneath the stage?" asked Holmes.

"Nothing. We waited for the trap to fall, but it didn't. So we eventually concluded that the trick had gone wrong - they do sometimes, you know and we went back on stage."

"And then?" prompted Holmes.

"And then, still nothing. Marvo's act was over and then we were told about the girl vanishing."

"So you didn't see anything of the princess under the stage?"

The other girl, Rose, said, "That's what Beth just told you, isn't it? In fact, we didn't see her at all, as we had to get under the stage before the volunteer came up from the audience."

"Nah, look 'ere, Mr Sherlock bloomin' 'Olmes, we've all told this already to the police. Can't you just go and look up our statements at the Yard?"

"My methods tend to be slightly different to

those applied by the police," my friend explained to the Chairman, "and, anyway, I like to see the scene of the crime at first hand and meet the participants."

"Who said it was a crime?" Mr Barker wanted to know.

"What else could it be?" responded Holmes, quite accurately in my judgement.

"Well, it might be someone pulling a joke," said Barker.

I exploded (metaphorically). "That is nonsense," said I.

The young lady on my arm, Tilly, looked up at my face (she was a mere slip of a thing) and murmured, "Do you know, I like a man with a moustache."

A silly play on words came back to me from my undergraduate days when I sometimes appeared with a bunch of fellows in a revue group, "No I don't," I said, very wittily, "but you hum it and I'll play it!"

I laughed at my sally, but the stupid girl just looked at me blankly. As did the rest of the assembled company. Some people simply have no sense of humour.

Even Holmes did not blink and eyelid at my witticism, which I explained at length to him after we had returned to Baker Street - but he still didn't understand it. He therefore ignored me and continued to talk to Alf Barker.

"Who else was in the music hall last night?"

"Now, that ain't all that easy to tell. I can tell you who was on the bill, but most of the artistes do two or three halls in one evenin' and the Stage Door looks like Waterloo in the rush hour most times, wiv people dashing in and out - some in costume, some half in and half out of costume and others off for the rest of the night. Then there's the mashers who hang around the Stage Door mostly after Ruby - Old Bert on the door ain't supposed to let 'em in, but if they tips enough... Well, yer've got to let nature take its course, ain't yer?"

"Who is Ruby?" asked Holmes.

"She's one of the chorus. She ain't 'ere. Gawd knows why not. Probably bin out too late last night with one of her blokes. Devil for the trousers is Ruby."

And the other girls all nodded and giggled a bit, while Tilly crept her hand up my arm to my face and stroked the ends of my moustache. I soon put a stop to that, of course.

"And then," went on Barker, "there's the stage hands and the orchestra, and the front of house people - you know, programme sellers, box office, bar staff - and then there was the audience. I should think there must have been upwards of six hundred and fifty people around at one time or other durin' the performance."

Holmes persisted. "I think we can discount anyone who was in front of the curtain from being involved in any way. Perhaps you can recall which individual acts should have been in the building at the time of the disappearance?"

Barker scratched his head. "Well, Johnny Wilson, the human xylophone, was the next act on after the girls' number, so he should have been here; and I know Joey Harris was here, 'cause he was too drunk to go on later and he'd been asleep in the scene dock; the Flyin' Zookinis was in as I saw 'em, all five of 'em, troop in while I was havin' my drink of water."

Pearl caught his eye and tossed her head.

"Anyone else?" asked my friend.

"Now there you 'ave me," Barker admitted. "The Family Klapp ain't got no other engagement, but it's all Lombard Street to a China Orange that

34

they was in their dressin' room, 'cause Maisie's expectin' again and tossing all them kids around on stage don't half take it out of her. A Song in the Air - cor, you'd think there was an easier way to make a livin', wouldn't yer?"

"Orpheus the Magnificent, the strong man, was over in the boozer with Billy Thimble, the clog dancer from Manchester," volunteered Beth.

"I imagine that the police have taken statements from all these people," Holmes said, "and I doubt if they can help very much. It seems to me that the whole operation was carried out on stage and anyone away from it - or even underneath it - could have played no part. Which of the stage hands was around at the time?"

"Again, it's difficult to say," said Barker. "Young Arfur was on the lightin' and someone was on the curtain. Who was on the tabs, girls?"

The chorus hadn't, it seemed, taken much notice of who was lifting and lowering the curtain for them, but Holmes said that he could easily find out later and passed on to other matters.

"Now," he went on, "Marvo was on stage, wasn't he?"

Barker cast his eyes to the heavens, "Cor, that goes without sayin'"

Pearl laughed out loud, "So did Tony's Performing Dogs: that's why we had to get rid of them."

Sherlock Holmes ignored this coarse interruption and asked, "Which of you knows anything about Marvo?"

Several of the girls claimed that they had worked at various halls at differing times with Marvo over the past few years, but none of them claimed any knowledge of the magician or his background. Barker knew Marvo's agent's address, but said he did not know where Marvo lived, even.

A man of mystery both on stage and off, it seemed.

There remained the man with white hair who had come from the audience to assist Marvo with his earlier trick, but again, none of the people assembled on stage before us, knew anything about him or what had happened to him after the disappearance. The general consensus was that he was probably a genuine member of the audience as, otherwise, the chances would have been that one of the chorus would have seen him as Marvo's accomplice somewhere previously.

I felt that we had learnt all there was to learn at this time and was trying to disengage my arm from that of my petite companion when another young lady rushed headlong on to the stage in a state of some déshabillé and pushed her way through to Alf Barker without so much as a glance at Holmes or myself.

The new arrival was a pretty little thing dressed in what is termed the height of fashion. She rushed over to Barker and announced that she was sorry she was late, but that she didn't care really; that she wasn't going to rehearse that day, as she was about to go off to see another friend; that she might or might not be around for the evening performances that night, and that someone would have to 'cover' for her; and that if Mr Alf Barker didn't like it, he could do something which I regarded as being anatomically impossible.

When she paused for breath, Tilly broke in, "Ruby! Quieten yourself! We've got visitors. This is Doctor Watson, the famous author, and that is Sherlock Holmes, the detective he writes about."

Holmes didn't take too kindly to this introduction I could see from his expression, but he persevered with his interrogation. "Miss, ah, Ruby. Were you at the hall last night?"

The young lady bobbed a curtsey. "Pleased to

meet you, I'm sure. My name's Blanchflower. And, yes, I was here last night."

"Where were you, then, when the disappearance took place?"

"I was in the dressing room with the others," Miss Blanchflower claimed.

"Oh, no, you wasn't," said Pearl.

"Oh, no, that's right. I was - helping one of my boy friends behind the scenes."

Alf Barker interrupted. He was still annoyed at the way Ruby had spoken to him when she had sailed in, I could see. "One of your boy friends! One of your boy friends! Which one?"

Lily Nightingale, who was standing next to Holmes whispered to him that Ruby was renowned - or, maybe, notorious - for the number of male admirers she had at her apron strings.

Ruby tossed her head at Barker. "What is it to you?" she asked.

Sherlock Holmes said, "If you could produce an alibi you could be eliminated from our enquiries, Miss Blanchflower."

"Ooo, don't he talk polite?" asked Pearl of nobody in particular.

"Well, then," said Ruby, "I was with Jimmy - he's a special friend of mine."

"And what were you doing?"

"The same as she does with Mickey and Freddy and Billy and Danny and Wally and Harry and Dickey and Ronnie and all the rest," interposed Pearl.

"It only goes to show," said Beth inconsequentially.

"Yes," said Pearl, "that's why she's got so many boy friends!"

Ruby went over to Pearl and, being a fairly small girl, looked up at her, saying, "Oh, I'll give your face such a smack!"

"Ladies! Ladies!" Holmes tried to bring their

attention back to the matter in hand. "Did you see anything that might help us in our investigation?"

"No," said Ruby. She turned abruptly away from Holmes and turned to Alf Barker. "Can't I go now? I'm late for a very important meeting already."

"Who's it with this time," asked Lottie. And the other chorus girls chipped in with various little queries like, "Who's your secret admirer?", "Is he handsome?" "Is he rich?" and so forth.

Ruby didn't take this in very good part and crossed to the small knot of girls. "That's for me to know and you to find out - if you dare," she grated at them.

Lily Nightingale tried to impose her authority on the chorus, "Girls, please, try to show a little decorum in front of Mr Holmes."

Ruby turned back towards us and apologised, "I'm sorry, but they keep picking on me. They're only jealous that I have that extra bit of something that they don't have."

Tilly whispered into my ear, "I've got a little bit of it too." But I pretended not to hear her.

"Do you want Ruby any more, Mr Holmes?" asked Miss Nightingale.

"I wouldn't wish to keep her from her appointment," Holmes said. "But I will need to talk to all of you at some other time, so I will expect to see her then."

"Run along then, Ruby," Alf Barker took control, "and if you don't show up tonight, I'll send a friend of mine round to break one of your legs. I don't mean that, 'f corse, Mr Holmes, just my fun."

Making what I considered to be a very rude gesture towards Pearl, Miss Ruby Blanchflower trotted off into the wings.

Holmes looked after her with a quizzical expression and then turned to Lily Nightingale, saying, "Does Ruby have a solo act of her own, by

38

any chance?"

"Yes," said Miss Nightingale, "how did you guess? She does a contortionist act - you know, juggling, balancing, somersaults, rolling herself into a ball, and that sort of thing."

Holmes seemed to have lost interest, not only in the answer to his last question, but in the music hall and his enquiry as a whole. Sometimes this happens, when he has assimilated as much information as he can digest. So I wasn't surprised when he announced, "Well, I won't detain you any longer from your rehearsal, Mr Barker."

To take the edge off Holmes' abrupt manner I said, picking up my bowler, "Thank you very much for your time, ladies. I enjoyed your dancing."

Tilly, still hanging on to my arm, murmured, "Come back to my dressing room and I'll really show you something!"

I must admit I was tempted; after all, there might have been something there relevant to our investigation. She pulled my arm and I made to follow her when Holmes cleared his throat rather obviously. I was reminded of my duty. "Can Mr Holmes come too?" I asked. For some reason Tilly let go my arm, stamped her foot and swept into the wings.

"Come along, old friend," said Holmes and we descended from the stage into the auditorium. I turned to wave farewell to the assembled company and cannoned into a saturnine figure who was walking towards the stage from the back of the theatre.

I was about to mutter my pardons, when Holmes exclaimed, "The Great Marvo, I presume?"

There was a stir among the people we had left back on stage and Lily Nightingale pushed her way to the footlights and peered over them, "Marvo, are you all right?"

The magician was surly, "All night long the police kept me. Sixteen hours. And I didn't have nothing to tell them. All I want to do is sleep!"

"Then why have you come here and not returned to your lodgings?" asked Holmes.

"'Cause my landlady won't have me back after being questioned by the police. She says there's no smoke without fire - stupid old -"

"Are you Marvo," I interrupted, "inventor of the Triple Coin Presentation?"

"Yes I am. And who might you be?"

From the stage Miss Nightingale said, "This is Mr Sherlock Holmes, the famous detective."

And Tilly, whose head had poked round from behind the scenes, added, "And Doctor Watson."

Marvo nodded to me, "Oh, yes, I've read your stories. I suppose this Sherlock bloke wants to ask me some more questions about the princess?"

Holmes is not used to being ignored in this way and snapped, "Yes. I would like to see how your trick was done."

"A magician doesn't reveal his tricks," Marvo drew himself up to his full height of some six feet, two inches. "And, anyway, I'm too tired to perform now. I suppose you still want me this evening?" and he turned to Alf Barker.

"Matinée too," Barker told him.

"Lor' lumee," groaned the magician, "I'll be dead on my feet."

"Come, Mr Marlow," said Holmes, "the sooner you answer my questions the sooner you can put your feet up prior to your performances."

"Yes, go on, Marvo," urged one of the chorus girls.

"A girl's life may hang on this", I pointed out.

"You don't have to go through the entire laughing act, does he, Mr Holmes?" intervened Barker.

"Of course not; he can still keep a few tricks up his sleeve, so to speak," Holmes smiled frostily.

"Well, I was doing that old favourite Homesick Jewels, I ask for a member of the audience who has a piece of jewellery - a broach, necklace, or something like that - to come up on stage. I then take the jewel and place it on a tailor's dummy; then the volunteer is covered in a silk cloth, the jewel vanishes from the dummy with a flash and, when the cloth is pulled off, the jewel is back in place on its owner."

I was fascinated. "How on earth do you manage that?"

"Basically it is sleight of hand. When the jewel is handed to me I palm it and substitute an imitation roughly made from silk and other combustibles which I put on the dummy. As I cover the person with the cloth I slip the real jewel back on to her and then, after a few 'magical incantations' the fake is set alight with a small electrical device in the dummy."

"But how," Holmes wanted to know, "do you know what jewel to make a copy of?"

"The volunteer from the audience is generally known to me."

"A stool pigeon?" I am quite proud of my command of lower class argot.

"Yes," the magician admitted. "But in this case I had been told that the princess was coming to the theatre and I made a copy of a jewel of hers that I had seen in *Illustrated London News.*"

"How could you be sure," pursued Holmes, "that the Princess would be the volunteer?"

"When I asked for someone to come up from the audience, I was looking straight at her - and few can resist such an invitation." Marvo preened himself, showing that he is a bounder of the first order.

41

"Then what happened when the Princess was on stage?" asked Holmes.

"Everything was as usual," said Marvo, "I exchanged the jewel, pinned the real brooch back on the girl, covered her with a black silk cloth, and turned away to set the electrical charge going. When I turned back the two girls - a couple of those up there, I think," he slightingly pointed at the chorus girls still grouped together on stage, "pulled the cloth forward and there she was - gone!"

Holmes shepherded Marvo and myself on to the stage. "Now, where was she standing exactly," he asked.

"Right here," indicated Marvo, pointing at a spot on the stage floor.

"Is there a trap there?"

"No," interrupted Alf Barker, "we've only got the one star trap, but that's over here." And he showed us the marks on the stage, fully three yards from where Marvo claimed the trick had been worked.

Holmes stood musing in the centre of the stage for a moment, then strode towards the back of the stage to whisk away the curtains there and reveal a bare brick wall.

As if thinking out loud he murmured, "And she can't have been hoisted into the flies or dived into the wings because the audience would have seen her."

"No one could have been more surprised than me," said Marvo. "I mean, I'm a magician, but I've never made anyone really disappear before. Weird, I calls it."

While this conversation had been going on the pit orchestra had been keeping themselves to themselves, possibly in the hope that they wouldn't be questioned, and at this moment they struck up a lively polka that reminded me of my student days.

Before I was troubled by my wound from the battle of Maiwand in Afghanistan in 1880, I was what was known in university dramatic circles as an eccentric dancer and could feel my feet irresistably tapping in time to the music.

"What on earth are you doing, Watson?" Holmes asked irrascibly.

"Come on, Doctor," shouted Tilly and she drew me into an energetic dance. At this all the chorus seemed to come alive and started clapping their hands and making 'whooping' noises. Holmes merely crossed his arms and looked down the length of his aquiline nose.

I performed to the best of my ability until suddenly my suspect leg gave way beneath me and I hurtled on to a small wooden box that had been sitting inconspicuously by the wings. My weight caused it to open out like a jack in the box's box and I sat there amidst its ruins feeling rather foolish. Meanwhile the chorus cheered and stamped their feet in mirth. I was touched when Holmes solicitously leaned over me and pulled me to my feet, murmuring, "Are you all right, old friend?"

As I was rising to my feet I was terribly embarrassed that Tilly, fundamentally the cause of my downfall, bestowed a very wet kiss on my cheek, saying as she did so that I was a 'game old bird'.

I apologised to Barker for destroying music hall property and Holmes said, "Let me pay for it. Would a sovereign cover it?"

Barker agreed that it would and, to my surprise, Holmes gathered up the pieces and put them under his arm. Clearly the examination of Marvo and the other music hall artistes was at an end as Holmes strode towards the steps leading from the stage. As he descended into the auditorium he thanked the cast for their time, indicating that he would return to continue the inquisition at some later date.

I followed Holmes into the auditorium, hotly aware that Tilly was blowing kisses at me and that this was making a couple of the other young ladies giggle.

In the hansom on the way back to Baker Street I offered to reimbuse Holmes for the pound that he had spent on the broken box, but he would have none of it, saying that it was worth it, simply to have the memory of my terpsichorean demonstration.

I sometimes suspect Holmes of being sarcastic.

THE CONSULTING ROOMS

THE CONSULTING ROOMS

When we got back to the rooms at Baker Street all I wanted to do, frankly, was rest. I had passed a strenuous early afternoon and I accordingly sat myself in the winged chair in front of the fireplace and composed myself for sleep.

Holmes, on the other hand, never rests when an investigation is in train. He immediately busied himself with his magnifying glass and started tinkering with the box I had flattened at the Hyperion.

I was drifting into somnulence, lulled by Holmes' background noises, when there was a tap on the door. In my chair I couldn't see who it was - but, then, neither could they see me!

Holmes went to the door and admitted the principal singer of the Hyperion, Lily Nightingale: I was relieved it was her rather than that Tilly, who was, I felt, rather a forward young miss.

"I showed myself up," said Miss Nightingale, "your housekeeper said she had something in the oven."

Holmes indicated that Miss Nightgale might sit down on the window seat.

"Well, just for a minute," said she, "I can't

stop long, but I've got something to tell you."

"I thought you had told me all you knew when we were in the music hall," said Holmes.

"Well, Sherlock - may I call you Sherlock?" simpered the young lady. Holmes seemed taken aback: to my knowledge he only allows his elder brother, Mycroft, the privilege of using his Christian name.

"Well, Sherlock, there is something I wanted to tell you, but with all those other girls around and that Alf Barker, I wasn't sure if I could talk in front of them."

"Why? Was it something confidential?"

"No, not really," said Miss Nightingale, "but I didn't want to seem to be too helpful with all those others around."

"I see," said Holmes. "What was it?"

"Do you live here on your own?" Miss Nightingale was on her feet, scanning the bookshelf by the door.

Holmes, never at his complete ease with the female sex, seemed discommoded. "Was that what you can here to ask?"

"No, but I just wondered. I've always thought you need a woman's touch around the home."

"Mrs Hudson, my housekeeper, cleans up once in a while and I have Doctor Watson for company."

"And I suppose you have lots of lady friends dropping in?" she asked coquettishly.

"I fail to see where this line of questioning is leading us. Normally I ask the questions." Holmes was getting quite brusque. I felt that this would not be a good time to reveal my presence, so I snuggled down into the chair, making myself even less obtrusive.

"I'm sorry," said Lily, "I've embarrassed you."

48

"Not at all," growled Holmes, "I appreciate your interest, but I really would like to know what you have come here this afternoon to tell me."

"Well," Lily was apparently going to unburden herself, "It was last night, when the disappearance was going on. I was in the dressing room."

"With the other girls," prompted Holmes.

"Yes," said Lily. And then I heard a small crash of glass. "Ooh, I am sorry," she exclaimed, "what have I done?"

Holmes went over to his chemistry table and I heard him mopping up a broken test tube and its contents, muttering that it didn't matter - or words to that effect.

Lily expressed interest in what all Holmes' apparatus was and he explained that, as part of his forensic investigations, he conducted a few simple experiments. She wanted to know if the box from the music hall, which, as I have indicated, was on Holmes' table, was one of his experiments.

Holmes said that he had observed a stain on its lid and that, as an incorrigible prier into things unknown to him, he was looking into it.

"However," he said sternly, "we are straying from the point again."

Lily apologised prettily, "It must be my theatrical blood. I was born in a trunk, as they say. My mother and father had a tumbling act, working terribly hard for a pittance. We were often 'resting', so I learnt what hardship was. I vowed I'd never be poor like them, but I'd have enough money to live life as it should be lived - to the full! There - I've uncovered my darkest secrets."

"We seem to be off the point yet again," Holmes is relentless when in search of evidence. "You did say that you had something to tell me about the disappearance."

"Well, I was in the dressing room, like I said, with the other girls and we heard a commotion that must have been when the Princess vanished. I was sitting nearest to the door and I heard the sounds of running footsteps."

"I imagine," said Holmes, "that it was someone running to find out what was the cause of the disturbance."

"But that's the point. The feet were running away from the stage, towards the stage door."

"Can you be certain of the direction?" asked Holmes.

"Yes, I've worked the Hyperion for some time now and you get used to the echoes backstage. They were a man's footsteps and he was wearing heavy shoes or boots."

"But how could he have got past the police or the stage door keeper without being seen?" enquired Holmes.

"I don't know. All I can tell you is what I heard."

"Very interesting. But I can't see why you couldn't have told me about this in front of the others."

Lily Nightingale didn't respond, but changed the subject again dramatically. "Excuse me, Sherlock, but - can I go and wash my hands, please?"

Holmes is like a hawk in investigation, but lacks the ability to understand polite euphonisms.

"I beg you pardon?" he stuttered.

"Can I wash my hands, please?" asked Lily.

"Oh, I see," light dawned on Holmes. "I do apologise. It's straight through the bedroom and on your right."

Lily thanked him and went into the bedroom. Holmes came over to me and asked what I made of this visit. I barely had time to whisper that I made nothing of it, when Lily was back and I sank back into the chair.

She still didn't notice me and said to Holmes, "I'm sorry to have taken up so much of your valuable time, but I've got to get back. We've got this matinée to get through."

"Not at all," sometimes Holmes retains a few of the social graces. "I was very interested to hear about your parents. Are they still alive?"

"No," said the girl, "my mother was run down by a horse omnibus and my father died while attempting a triple back somersault."

Holmes asked what had happened.

"He missed the stage and landed in the kettle drum in the orchestra pit. He always did want to go out with a bang," and she laughed. "I'm sorry, Sherlock, but you see what I mean about us theatricals always making light of our disasters."

Holmes seemed a bit put out. Being humorous in the face of death is not his way. His manner was withdrawn as he said, "And have you anything more to tell me about the Princess Fatima's disappearance?"

"I'd like to stay and have a chat, Sherlock, but I simply must dash. Alf'll have my scalp if I'm late for my entrance. And I've got this new costume that I've got to get into. And I've got to get my war paint on. Got to go!"

I am largely unacquainted with the young ladies of the stage so I was surprised to hear my bachelor friend receive a thorough-going kiss just before the door slammed to behind our visitor.

"We didn't learnt a great deal from that, did we?" commented Holmes as I rose from my chair.

I slyly remarked, "Well, not about the case, anyway." And Holmes blushed, a sight I cannot recall seeing at any previous time.

Holmes settled down again with his

magnifying glass and the music hall box and I picked up the *Morning Post*, which had been neglected since it arrived. There is a lot of sensationalism getting into the newspapers these days, simply encouraging the criminal classes to greater feats of daring. If one gang learns through the penny press that Lord So-and-So has been burgled, it seems to inspire them to emulate the example of their peers and burgle another member of the House of Lords in their turn.

In the newspaper I was perusing, for example there was a report of a burglary at Lord Chumley's town house in Belgrave Square. Apparently he had been said to be in Scotland for the season, but had returned unexpectedly to an empty house to find a team of burglars filching the family silver. One of the gang had been caught by the constabulary, but the others had got away by jumping on to the back of a passing hackney carriage.

The *Post* reporter claimed that this was the work of an organised gang who had been operating throughout the West End for some time. The police, it was said, had very few leads even though they had caught this one miscreant: he wouldn't, in American parlance, talk.

Also in the newspaper there were reports of the return of the last of our brave boys from the South African campaign and of the laying down of a new battleship in Jarrow. There was some social chit-chat of people with more money and leisure than sense in Biarritz, but none of this gripped my imagination and I was aware that I was letting the newspaper slowly fall to the floor before being taken into the arms of Morpheus.

When I awoke, Sherlock Holmes was still busy at his table, but had now abandoned his magnifying glass for a scalpel and test tube. He had scraped something, as far as I could judge, from the inside of the music hall's box and was subjecting this to analysis.

"Ah, there you are, Watson," Holmes greeted my return to consciousness affably.

"How is the investigation going, Holmes?" I enquired.

"The investigation. Yes. The investigation." Holmes seemed to muse. "If I'm not mistaken...

I interposed, "And you very rarely are!"

"Thank you, Watson. If I'm not mistaken we have seen a number of scarlet fish."

"I beg your pardon, old man?"

"Scarlet fish. Red herrings." Holmes really has a most elementary sense of humour. "Consider this, here we have a magician who cannot apparently control his own tricks, young ladies who can't see what is happening under their noses and yet everyone seems very willing to talk and talk and talk."

"And what about Lily Nightingale?" I posed.

"What indeed." Holmes went into a small reverie. "A fascinating woman, Watson. She reminds me of - but no matter. There is more to this case than meets the eye. We shall have to tread very carefully in this case."

"What case? D'you mean this old box?" I asked.

"No, Watson. I meant the investigation. However, I have to say that this old box does have some interest. Do you see the stain that is on the inside of the lid?" And Holmes indicated with his right forefinger the area he was examining. "I've run a few experiments on it and it appears to be greasepaint of a common brand used by the theatre people."

I was bound to point out that all that proved was that the box was around the theatre and used by a member of the company and that that was self-evident, even to me. It is not often that I can show

Holmes that some of his experiments are unnecessary in the face of good common sense, but just as I was about to explain myself even further, there was a knock at the door and Mrs Hudson pushed into the room an urchin, who had clearly recently washed his face and hands (although not his neck!).

Sherlock Holmes bent down to examine our new visitor and exclaimed, "Why! It's young Joe, our bootblack boy. This just shows, Watson, how little one needs to do to effect a passable disguise. Joe here is almost unrecognisable having been introduced to soap!"

The young man drew himself to the full height of his four feet three inches and said, "I'm 'ere on official business and I'm goin' to be a detective like you when I grow up; so I thought I'd better posh meself up a bit." Then Joe relaxed a bit and cheekily said, "And the lady wot give me this said I had to clean meself afore I come 'ere, anyway."

"Well, Joe," said Holmes in an amused voice, "what have you brought me?"

"This lady give me this bowl of eggs to give to you and said you'd give me 'alf a crown for 'em."

This seemed a very enterprising way of obtaining an exhorbitant price for eggs to me and I said as much, but Holmes shushed me and turned back to Joe.

"Who was this lady?"

"I never saw her before, but she was in a cloak and bonnet. She had nice hands too." Joe turned to me and said, "My big bruvver has read me all your stories about that detective bloke and how you've got to observe all the time."

I was pleased that Joe had assimilated my exposition of Holmes' methods, although Holmes himself did not seem very appreciative.

54

"Who did she say you had to deliver these eggs to?" he asked.

"Number 221B Baker Street and ask the lady to show me to the tall thin geezer wot lives on the first floor wiv Doctor Watson - that's you, ain't it?" Joe turned to me yet again.

I admitted the charge, but almost spoilt the moment by having to choke a laugh into my handkerchief, after having seen Holmes' reaction to being described simply as someone 'wot lives' with me. In my bonhomie I flicked half a sovereign to Joe - an extravagance I would regret later, but it seemed worth it at the time.

"Cor, thanks, mister," gasped the boy and, before I might change my mind, he dashed out of the door, pushing Mrs Hudson rather rudely to one side. She bridled and went out muttering something about the 'younger generation having no respect for their elders'.

"I hope, Watson, that you have spent ten shillings wisely," observed my friend, "Let's have a look at these eggs."

Holmes picked them over one by one, shaking them close to his ear as he did so. Without understanding what he was doing, but willing to learn from his example, I did the same.

"I suspect that one of these eggs will contain some relevant information," said Holmes.

I asked him what he meant.

"There is an old trick by which you can write on the inside of an egg. What you do is to dissolve an ounce of alum with half a pint of vinegar. You take this and, using it as an ink, write on the shell of an egg with a pointed brush. Then all you do is boil the egg for some fifteen minutes and the lettering will disappear from the shell. But - and this is the clever part - when the egg is broken open the message appears on the hard-boiled white."

I was amazed. Experimentally I tapped one egg open, but for my pains all I got was far from fresh egg all over my hands. Dripping egg yolk and white I excused myself and went into Holmes' bedroom where there was a water jug in which I could rinse my hands.

I completed my ablutions and was drying my hands on a towel preparatory to returning to further assist my friend when something dropped, seemingly from the sky, on to my left shoulder. I stole a glance at the object and nearly had a seizure. On my shoulder, flicking its tongue in and out in a very suggestive way, was a small black snake. I have never been described as a nature lover and I rate snakes far below most other animal forms; this specimen, I decided, was not desirable. I emitted a strangled yelp and dashed back into Holmes' presence.

Holmes, already bent back at the bowl of eggs, did not even glance up. "What's the matter, old chap?" he enquired casually.

I was bereft of speech, but managed to gurgle a further half scream, which did attract Holmes' attention. He looked up and saw my incubus; he mouthed at me to stay still - which was not difficult for I was well nigh paralysed with fright - and slowly moved to the fireplace where he selected a poker from among the fire irons. He then as slowly moved across the room towards me, then, with a sudden flick, removed the snake from my shoulder and, in the same movement, stamped on its head with the heel of his shoe.

As I sank shakily into my chair he simply returned the poker to its place among the tongs, saying, "You had a lucky escape there, Watson."

I leaned from my chair and poured myself a stiffish whiskey from the decanter on the side table, topping it up with a squirt from the gazogene.

I sipped the restorative and croaked, "Thanks, old man, you saved my life."

"That is a much over-worked phrase, Watson, but in this case you could well be right. One bite from that beast could have meant death."

"But whoever planted it in your bedroom must have meant it for you," I pointed out. "Do you think someone is trying to kill you?"

"No," said Holmes, "whoever left that snake there simply intended it as a calling card to let me know that they have been studying my movements in close detail."

"What do you mean," I asked. "If the animal could have killed me, it could have killed you with equal ease, surely?"

"Not so," said Holmes. "You will probably recall that trip I made up the Amazon with the British Scientific Expedition in February and March this year? When I was in a tributary of the Obamza River I was bitten by a similiar snake. Luckily these beasts are endemic to the region and the party carried the antidote serum: its effects are known to be active for up to six months, so whoever planted this snake knew that, although it might have given me a nasty time, the effects would not have been fatal. You would not have been so immune, old friend."

"The only visitor we have had and therefore the only person who could have planted it has been..." But Holmes interrupted me with a pleasurable cry.

"This is the egg!" Quickly he stripped it of its shell and there, sure enough, was faint printing in block capitals on the surface of the white. "YOUR ANSWER LIES IN THE DEN OF THIEVES IN SOHO." In another hand, as far as I could judge, there was a postscriptum, "P.S. BEWARE OF SNAKE."

Speaking for myself I was amazed and I

could see that Holmes was equally bereft of speech, though, in his case, I image that he might simply have been thinking hard. When I recovered from my surprise, I seized the egg from Holmes' fingers. "And do you mean to say," I demanded, "that this is just an ordinary egg?" And, almost without thinking I bit into the object. I regretted this immediately as my entire mouth seemed to shrink in and I became as dry as an Afghan wadi.

Holmes smiled his superior smile, "Yes, Watson, alum has a nasty taste. Someone must have have over-alummed the egg."

I gasped out to Holmes what I should do to alleviate the discomfort, but as I did there was a tap on the door and Holmes wheeled towards it, saying, "Come in, Lestrade."

Sure enough, when the door opened there was Inspector George Lestrade, with an aggressive Mrs Hudson behind him. "Wipe your feet before you go in. I don't know," she grumbled, "this place is getting like Piccadilly Circus, what with people popping in and popping out. And don't you keep Mr Holmes too long, he's a busy man - even if you aren't!"

She swept off downstairs, muttering about her baking being interrupted and policemen's big boots and various other matters that were disturbing her equanimity.

I choked out a greeting to the Inspector and Holmes, remembering my predicament, turned to me and advised me to pour myself a carbonated water and drink it slowly. Then he briskly turned back to Lestrade. "Now, Lestrade, I assume you've got something to tell me about the Princess's disappearance?"

"In a manner of speaking, yes," replied the Inspector, who then caught sight of the mangled snake on the hearthrug. "Great Scotland Yard!" he exclaimed. "What's that snake doing here?"

"If it is dead - nothing," Sherlock Holmes tartly answered. "Now, what about the Princess?"

"The Commissioner personally asked me to take charge of the case," boasted Lestrade.

"But my information is that she disappeared in front of your eyes - almost within touching distance of you. I am surprised that in the circumstances the Commissioner has not got you directing traffic in St Giles Circus at this very moment."

Lestrade was not amused and chose to ignore the slight. "Even though I saw it with my own eyes, I still can't believe it. I mean to say, people just don't disappear into thin air. It's a puzzle."

"Every puzzle must have a solution," Holmes remarked, rather pompously, I thought. My mouth was feeling much easier after having swilling liquid round it.

"The Commissioner agrees with you, Mr Holmes, and that is why he has asked me to ask you to step along with me to the Yard for questioning."

There was a pause while the import of that remark sunk in, I responded first, "Surely you don't think that Holmes had anything to do with this business, do you?"

"My personal opinion of of no consequence," Lestrade could be pompous in his turn, "but we must investigate every avenue. There are the facts that Mr Holmes fits the description of the man seen at the scene of the disappearance and that we have recovered a deerstalker hat from an unused dressing room at the theatre."

Holmes seemed to be amused, "But you can see my hat from here, Inspector. That's it, hanging on the door."

Lestrade observed in a gruff voice that hats could be replaced if mislaid.

59

I felt bound to intervene, "This whole thing is ridiculous. Any fool can wear a deerstalker. Why, hats like that are ten a penny."

"You are indulging in hyperbole, Watson, but you have to believe, Lestrade, that this 'fool' has not purchased a new hat in five years. Ask Mrs Hudson."

"Look, I'm sorry, Mr Holmes. I've worked with you on many occasions and I know you wouldn't be involved in any crime from the other side in fact," Lestrade added, "you're the straightest man I have ever met. But I've still got my orders to take you in - just for questioning, you understand."

I tried to make sense of all this. "If you know that he's innocent, why waste your time doing all this? Why don't you go out and catch the real criminals?"

"My personal feelings don't come into this, Doctor," Lestrade almost sighed, "I've got to ask you to come along with me, Mr Holmes."

As Lestrade stepped forward as if to grasp Holmes by the shoulder I realised I had to intervene. I threw myself into a fighting pose and waved my fists in Lestrade's face. "Take one step further," I glowered, "and I'll punch you in the nose!"

Lestrade bristled at me, "Are you threatening an Officer?"

"Gentlemen, gentlemen," my maligned friend tried to pour oil on our storm in a teacup, "I understand your feelings, Watson, but, as Lestrade says, orders is orders. I will be happy to accompany you, Inspector. I don't suppose it will take all that long?"

"Of course not, Mr Holmes, it's a mere formality."

"If it's a formality," I grumbled, "it all seems a bally waste of time."

Holmes was looking round the room,

searching for something, I could tell. Meanwhile he continued to chat, "I hear that you're going to retire next year, Lestrade."

"I have plans to set up a private detective agency, Mr Holmes. Upon your model, of course."

I snorted. This syncophant was thinking to take his 'model' in for questioning!

"Oh, dear," sighed Holmes, "I seem to have mislaid my pipe. I'll just fetch it from the other room." And he went into the bedroom humming to himself.

In Holmes' absence I felt constrained to point out to Lestrade that I thought he was making a fool of himself and, thus, of the rest of the Metropolitan Police. Lestrade had the grace to look abashed and he wandered over to the mantlepiece trying to avoid catching my eye.

"Hey," he shouted, "isn't this Mr Holmes' pipe?" And he flourished my friend's calabash. "'Ere, wait a minute!" Lestrade rushed across the room, flung open the bedroom door and charged into Holmes' private room. He reappeared in a matter of seconds, looking very stern. "He's gone. He's done a runner. He's slipped out on the balcony and over into next door," he announced, putting a police whistle to his lips.

Before he could blow it to summon assistance I flung myself on him, grasping him firmly around the knees - a movement I remember from my school days in Edinburgh when I played Rugby - and throwing him to the ground.

For a few moments all was confusion with Lestrade lashing out in every direction, while I tried to restrain him. We eventually landed up with me sitting on his chest - I think I have a few pounds avoirdupois advantage over him.

"Let go of me," bellowed my fallen adversary, "You're only making things worse."

I merely crossed my arms and tried to make myself heavier by thought processes.

In the event this gesture was rather silly as Lestrade was able to manoeuvre under me and, while my hands were unavailable, he levered himself into a position of throwing me off, as he did so punching me, most unsportsmanlike, in the abdomen.

As I lay gasping on the floor, in my turn, Lestrade retrieved his whistle, blew loudly on it and, as he raced through the door and down the stairs, I could heard him shouting, "Arrest Holmes! Stop him! I'll get him if it's the last thing I do!"

I had given Holmes a few seconds extra start, but I had to admit to a great disturbance of mind. Why had Holmes run from the law? Was he implicated in the disappearance of the Princess? How could I get his pipe to him?

THE DEN OF THIEVES

THE DEN OF THIEVES

I spent the rest of that afternoon in a daze, mulling over and over in my mind what could have possessed Sherlock Holmes to turn into a fugitive from the law. There was no possibility that he had committed any crime, so why had he escaped from Lestrade in the way he had? As an outlaw, what, I wondered, would he do now? Where was he?

I resolved that in Holmes' absence I was honour bound to pursue enquiries about the missing princess and, as I saw it, the best place was the Hyperion. I accordingly made my way to the Strand and gained admittance to the music hall mid-way through the first half of their early evening performance.

I saw on the placards as I entered the foyer that the Great Marvo now had top billing, displacing 'the Scottish nightingale', Hettie McCrum. Clearly the Hyperion was cashing in on its new found notoriety. I wondered if Marvo would descend to his usual place on the bill when the present nine days' wonder was over.

The girl at the Box Office said that the place was packed and that no seats were available, but I brushed her aside, saying that I was investigating the mystery and that I would find myself a place somewhere inside. So saying, I stepped through into the auditorium to observe that the girls of the chorus - among whom I picked out Tilly - were performing an energetic dance that seemed to involve displaying a prodigious amount of underwear to an appreciative audience.

The exhibition terminated by the girls throwing themselves, one after another, into the position known as the 'splits', gaining them substantial applause and ear-piercing whistling from the onlookers.

Alf Barker was in his habitual position at his table by the side of the stage, a flask of water by left hand and a gavel, which he now used vigorously to restore order, in his right.

"Thank you, gentlemen," he bawled, "and thank you, the Hyperion girls - weren't they lovely, ladies and gentlemen?"

This question brought a noisy response and Barker held up his white-gloved hands in mock surrender, "I'll let you see a bit more of the girls later." This slightly ambiguous statement drew forth a storm of good natured cat-calls and whistling from the crowd - as I have no doubt Barker had expected.

"And now," he continued, "my favourite and your favourite, the girl with the golden larynx, the delectable chanteuse who has stolen all our hearts - Miss Lily Nightingale!"

Miss Nightingale, dressed in a demure cotton frock and a poke bonnet, came on stage to rapturous applause and sang a very pleasing love song. It was so unlike the previous number that I had heard her render - the rather raucous item about the railway porters - that I could scare believe it was the same young lady. Clearly Lily Nightingale had more to her than appeared at first glance.

I inched my way towards the stage and, by

the time the singer had finished her melody and had curtseyed to the applause I was standing by the steps leading on to the performance area.

Alf Barker banged with his gavel as the applause died down and shouted, "And now, my lords, ladies and gentlemen, now comes the time you have all been waiting for! I am pleased to announce the Hyperion's famous and celebrated - interval!" So saying, he brought his gavel down again and left the stage, cheerily mopping a streaming brow as he did so.

I was not aware of the customs of the music hall and was surprised that most of the chorus girls issued from back stage into the auditorium and mingled with the audience. Clearly the Hyperion had a free and easy atmosphere. I was quite flattered when Miss Nightingale approached me, although she might well have been put off by the expression on my face, which must have been dour from her first words.

"A penny for them, Doctor Watson?"

I muttered something about 'being miles away' and I offered her a drink, which she refused saying that she never imbibed while she was working. My opinion of Miss Nightingale rose, as she must be subject to many temptations in this milleu.

"Are you worried about Sherlock's disappearance?" she asked. Bad news, I reflected, travels fast.

I admitted that I was, pointing out that I had no doubts about his integrity and that he must have had a compelling reason to do what he had done. I complimented her on her singing of her ballad, but admitted that my main reason for coming to the music hall had been to search for more clues about the princess - who seemed to have become less important since Holmes' own vanishing trick.

Lily meltingly said, "I found Sherlock a most fascinating man. Although I only spent a few minutes alone with him, I felt his intellectual force most strongly. I am looking forward to meeting him again - perhaps in a happier situation."

I was about to admit that I had overheard her interview with Holmes and to question her about the snake, when I was pleasantly aware of being hugged from behind by a young lady. It was Tilly, who I had met previously.

She was effusive at seeing me, "Hello, Doctor, what are you doing here?"

"He's come to investigate the disappearance again," explained Lily, who then turned to me, saying, "Excuse me, Doctor Watson, I've got this other costume to get into for the next item after the break. It's a bit difficult and we don't run to dressers at the Hyperion. See you later." And she was off in a flurry of skirts.

Tilly hung on to my arm as if I might be going to follow Lily and asked if I had any theories about either disappearance. I was bound to say that my notebook was blank, but that I hoped to rectify that now.

"Have you seen over back stage, Doctor?" asked my companion. "Here, come with me and I'll show you round."

We went through a pass door from the auditorium to the wings of the stage and Tilly, holding close to my arm the while, quickly showed me the lighting board and the scenery stacked at the side of the stage. We peered into the gloom of the fly tower, where the back-cloths were stored prior to being dropped in when needed. She conducted me down the corridor off which were the dressing rooms and the toilets and then we descended underneath the stage where we looked at the trap and its safety landing - a big sort of pillow which would break the fall of anyone should the trap door open unexpectedly.

I disengaged myself from the girl to stoop to examine this item more closely, as I still felt that there was a possibility that the missing Princess might have left the stage abruptly downwards.

No clue manifested itself and, when I straighted up, I was startled to see Tilly with her hands behind her back, apparently undoing the fastenings of her costume.

"Come over here and help me, doctor dear," she said.

I was unsure what course of action to pursue, but gallantry overcame hesitation and I went over to her.

"Just that bottom hook," Tilly pointed. I undid it and she stepped out of her dress, letting it fall to the floor. She crossed to the trap pillow and reclined upon it, patting a place by her side to invite me to join her. "It's all right. Nobody's going to come down here until Marvo's act in about three quarters of an hour. I've got a lot of things I'd like to show you."

As an officer and a gentleman I prefer not to go into details of the following half an hour, except to say that it had no relevance to my investigation of the missing princess, although it was most revealing in a number of other ways.

When I took my leave of Tilly I did not feel inclined to conduct any further investigations at the theatre, so I saw myself out through the Stage Door and began to wend my way back to Baker Street in a thoughtful mood.

I wandered through Covent Garden, past Seven Dials and into Tottenham Court Road in a brown study, occasionally bumping into other pedestrians, although I remembered to mumble apologies for so doing. I turned into the Marylebone

Road and, having walked past Holy Trinity Church and across the bottom of Regents' Park, I was approaching Baker Street, when I walked full tilt into an oncoming pedestrian. He recovered first.

"Doctor Watson, I presume?" Lestrade tipped his bowler at me in what I considered to be an insolent manner. "I was hoping I'd run into you."

As my thoughts, such as they were, would have consigned Lestrade to territories unknown to the Metropolitan Police, I did not share his hope and said so.

Lestrade was apologetic, "Come now, Doctor, you know I'm only doing my job."

I ungraciously admitted that was true.

Lestrade continued, "And you must agree that Mr Holmes' running away like that was suspicious. I mean to say, would an innocent man escape over a balcony like that?"

I indicated that I considered that my friend must have had a good reason for his actions.

"Well, whether he's innocent or not, we'll soon catch him. Scotland Yard's methods are infallible."

I resisted the temptation to recall to the Inspector the numerous times when Holmes had corrected the Yard's 'infallible methods' or draw his attention to various unsolved crimes that I knew of that had failed to respond to these same methods.

"If, Doctor, you have any information that could lead to Mr Holmes' apprehension, I would suggest you let us know. Withholding information from the police is a criminal matter, you understand."

I was not going to co-operate. "I only wish I did know something," I snapped, "it would then give me great pleasure not to tell you!"

Lestrade was not amused, "Don't take that tone with me, Doctor. You're lucky I didn't arrest you this morning for obstructing an Officer in the course of his duty."

"I've told you before that you'd be better employed in looking for whoever kidnapped this Princess Fatima."

Lestrade sneered - positively sneered - "And what makes you think we aren't?"

A man can take just so much. At this cool effrontery, which I regarded as an insult to my friend, I adopted a pose prelimary to knocking the bounder down.

Lestrade took a step backwards and raised his hand, "Just you take a swing at me and I'll run you in! My patience won't take much more of this. It's only our past relationship that stops me taking you in for questioning already. If you do hear anything I would seriously advise you to let me know. You know where you can contact me: the telephone number is Whitehall 1212."

He strode off muttering angrily to himself. In my turn I crossed the road, avoiding a motor car, and stormed up Baker Street, blind to other passers by.

I reached 221B and was fumbling for my latchkey when I was hailed from the area below. It was Mrs Hudson, who stiffly climbed up the area steps to my level.

"Good afternoon, Doctor, I'm just off to do some shopping. That Inspector Lestrade was round here a few minutes ago casting aspersions on Mr Holmes. Very unlike him."

"I don't understand it," I said, "Lestrade seems to be convinced that Mr Holmes was involved in the kidnapping of that Princess."

"I know," said Mrs Hudson, "I told him he was barmy. But I do wish I knew where Mr Holmes was. I do get so awfully worried... the thought of him out there somewhere..."

Mrs Hudson started sobbing. If there is one thing I cannot cope with it is women in tears, so I tried to rally her. "I am certain that wherever he is he can take good care of himself. And I am sure that we'll hear from him soon. Now, don't distress yourself, Mrs Hudson, no news is good news, you know."

Comforted by my platitude, Mrs Hudson went on her way and I let myself into the house, plodding up the stairs to Holmes' flat weary in body and soul. Getting to the top of the stairs, I paused for I thought I heard movement within.

I flung open the door and there, crouched on the floor in front of Holmes' filing cabinet, was a scruffy looking person in blue seaman's rig, with a cap pulled down over his forehead. Without a second's hesitation I threw myself upon him and, aided by superior weight, managed to pin him to the floor.

"Now, you bounder," I panted, "what are you doing here? You leave Holmes' things alone."

The miscreant, cowed by my bearing, put up no defence, "It's a fair cop, guv'nor," he whined, "please don't hand me over to the rozzers, I've got a wife and ten children to support. I was desperate. Say you won't shop me."

"Indeed I will," I said, leaving aside the problem of how I was going to keep the fellow under my control while getting help from outside. "Trying to make off with the belongings of Sherlock Holmes."

The criminal cringed even further, "Sherlock Holmes! Cor, if I'd known it was his gaff I'd never have broken in. 'Struth, I'm a great admirer of his 'cause of those wonderful stories in the *Strand* written by that brilliant author, Doctor Watson. 'Ere! You wouldn't be him, would you?"

I admitted the character and, feeling that

it would be churlish to continue to fetter the good fellow, I released my hold on him.

"Blimey, may I shake you by the 'and, guv'nor? Lummee, this'll be something to tell the missus about when I gets home."

I permitted the man, who I now noticed was quite a respectable sort of chap, really, to pump my hand up and down fairly vigorously.

"'F course," he said, "we have met before."

I said that I had no recollection of such a meeting, but he insisted. I racked my brains, but could not call him to mind. Of course, I do meet a great number of disreputable persons in my exploits with Holmes and when I ran a medical mission in the East End in the early nineties, when Holmes was missing after the Reichenbach Falls episode, I ran across many more. This artisan was probably one of my patients at that time.

I put this to him, but he shook his head.

"No, sir," said he, "I've seen you since then. Often."

"Sorry, m'dear fellow, "can't recall you at all."

"But you must," said the fellow, taking off his cap. I was struck by his piercing blue eyes. "Surely you do," he went on, removing a walrus moustache.

"Great bugs of Barnet," I exclaimed, "Holmes!"

Holmes, for it was none other than he, laughed and said, "Well, if I fooled you, I may stay out of the clutches of Scotland Yard for a few more hours."

"But why did you escape?" I asked.

"I knew that if I had gone with Lestrade I could easily have proved an alibi, but that would have taken time and I can't afford to waste any of that precious commodity in futile questioning."

73

"So you adopted this disguise," I prompted.

"Do you remember the alum egg?"

I pulled a wry face, "I will not forget that in a hurry."

"You will recall the message. The answer lies in the Den of Thieves in Soho. So I have donned a suitable disguise that I hope will be accepted amongst the stews of London. If I can break into their circle I may be able to rescue the Princess and foil a plot that I am beginning to suspect may have further ramifications."

"But," I protested, "there must be hundreds of dens of thieves in London and dozens in Soho alone."

"The message said The Den of Thieves, so I am hopeful that there is one particular hang out of the criminal fraternity that is specifically called that."

"You mean like a pub?"

"Well," said Holmes, smiling, "hardly a pub, but something along those lines. More like a criminal club, I suspect."

While I accepted all that I still could not see how Holmes was going to discover this location amongst London's underworld and said so.

"I'm going to put it about that I'm looking for some dirty work to do and see if that'll lead me to the haunt. And I want your help, old man."

"Mine?" I was flattered that Holmes knew he could rely on me.

I was about to ask how I could be of assistance when the door opened and Mrs Hudson walked in carrying a handful of post, which she dropped on Holmes' desk with barely a glance at either of us. "Oh, good afternoon, Mr Holmes," she said casually.

I was astounded. "You recognised him?", I spluttered.

"Course I did. I know all Mr Holmes' faces. And I've seen his Lascar disguise before."

"Didn't fool me either," I bluffed. "Well, maybe just for a couple of seconds."

Sherlock Holmes laughed as heartily as I have heard him. "Perhaps Mrs Hudson and I can work miracles of disguise upon you too, old friend."

"I beg your pardon," I enquired, "what do you mean?"

"I need a trusty arm by my side when I venture into Soho and there is nobody on whom I can better rely than John Watson."

I swelled with pride to hear these words. Sherlock Holmes does not give compliments lightly.

"But," he went on, "you look a bit too much like the good chap you are. But we can soon alter that. Sit down over here. And, Mrs Hudson, fetch your scissors, please."

I sat down gingerly on one of our dining chairs, as indicated, and wondered what was going to happen to my appearance. Mrs Hudson came in with some scissors and Holmes said to her, pointing at my moustache, "Get it off!"

I clasped my hand across my upper lip. "Never," I mumbled through my fingers, "it has taken years of careful cultivation to get this moustache to its present growth. You shan't clip it."

"Not even to rescue an Arabian Princess from a fate possibly worse than death, Watson?"

I reluctantly withdrew my hand and, in a matter of seconds, Mrs Hudson had me cropped as close as a sheep after shearing.

"Good. Now get these on, please." Holmes threw a bundle of clothing into my lap. "Come on. Quickly."

With dignity I asked Mrs Hudson to leave the room, which she did with an expression on her

75

face that I can only describe as a smirk.

I divested myself of my usual apparel and put on the rig that Holmes had given me. It was generally on the lines of his own outfit and I began to fancy myself as a mercantile blade. When I was dressed Holmes sat me down in the chair again and applied a liquid to my face. I endured this stoically, but was disappointed when I looked in the hand mirror he then passed me. I may not be handsome, but I have always thought myself to be distinguished. Now I looked disreputable.

"Right," said Holmes, "now your name is Abe Slaney and you have just got back from the West Indies with me. Unfortunately, you are dumb - because try as you will you couldn't disguise your voice - so I treat you as a faithful follower, giving you orders, but expecting no reply."

I resented Holmes' slight upon my acting ability, but probably he was right. I have trusted Holmes to the death before, so I saw no reason to query his decision as to my identity now.

"Oh," Holmes remembered, "I forgot your shoes." He got out from his cabinet a pair of the biggest boots I have ever seen. "Try these on for size."

To my surprise they almost fitted. With the addition of some screwed up newspaper they were almost comfortable. But their weight! It felt as if I was a deep sea diver with lead weights in my boots to keep me from floating to the surface. I could only hope that no fleetness of foot would be wanted in the near future.

"Come along, Abe," said Holmes. He repeated this with some asperity before I realised he was talking to me.

We clomped out and downstairs, calling our farewells to Mrs Hudson as we went. She called back, wishing us well and asking Holmes to look after me! I did not know whether to be touched by her concern or annoyed at her lack of faith in my own abilities.

By a circuitous route we got to Soho and then plodded the pavements for what seemed like hours, Holmes barely glancing up and never addressing a word to me. I was, of course, not allowed to speak to him, so it was all pretty miserable. It came on to rain, a persistent rain that soaked us both within fifteen minutes, and with the rain dusk fell.

I am not very familiar with the Soho area of London as it is not safe to walk the streets casually in the ordinary way. I was interested to look around me at the down and outs propped in doorways, at costermongers plying their trades, at Jewish shopkeepers standing in the doorways of their tailors' shops, at policemen walking in pairs, at ladies of easy virtue hanging out of windows and bawling at us as we shuffled past, at Italian mommas, and at the dregs of every nationality under the sun all of whom seemed to have congregated in this quarter of London.

We had progressed along Great Compton Street, turning north into Wardour Street, then into a portal of hell called St Anne's Passage, and then into an even more disreputable alley, when Holmes turned a corner and walked straight into a very rough diamond indeed. This individual jumped back and, quicker than my eye could observe, had a knife in his hand.

Holmes was placatory. "Sorry, guv', no offence! My fault."

"Alright," muttered the tough grudgingly, "but you watch where you're goin'. Where **was** you goin', anyway? There's nothin' down 'ere."

"We're seamen not long in port and I've heard a whisper there's some easy money to be made round here," said Holmes.

"Money's never easy to come by, mister," growled the tough.

"Maybe you ain't lookin' in the right places, mate. I'm lookin' for the Den of Thieves. Heard of it?" Holmes enquired.

"No, I 'aven't. And I wouldn't ask too many questions round 'ere if I was you. See?"

"Thanks, guv," responded Holmes.

The gentleman who had been so quick on the draw with his knife departed with an almost friendly wave and we stood undecided what to do next. From a doorway stepped a young lady who I half recognised in the dim light of the alley.

"Hey, mister," said called - and I remembered where I had seen her before. This was Ruby, the girl who had many boy friends from the Hyperion Theatre. "Hey, mister, did I hear you say you're after some easy money?"

"I'm lookin' to get it - not spend it," Holmes rudely said to her. He can be quite coarse when in character.

"I'm not on the game, dearie. But I know where you can find the Den of Thieves."

Holmes asked if she could take us there and she came right over to us and looked at both of us keenly. Then she linked arms with Holmes and me and, saying to come along, propelled us back down the alley.

At the end we swung left and about three doors down this new alley, she let go of us to rap on a door fronting immediately on to the footpath. A grill on the door drew back and a suspicious pair of eyes peered out. Seeing Ruby, the grill shut and the whole door opened. As we followed Ruby in, the doorman barred our way, "Who's this, then?" he asked our escort.

"Two new members of the gang - at least,

they want to be."

"Don't be daft. We don't want new members."

Ruby persisted, "That's all you know, Mister Clever. I can always do with a new member. And the Boss will be pleased with these two, you'll see."

The man at the door was still inclined to argue. "But we don't know nuffin' about 'em. They could be anyfink. Might even be plain clothes coppers!"

"Don't take on so, Tom," said Ruby, "they're only just off a ship."

"What ship," Tom wanted to know.

"If you really have to know," grumbled Holmes, "the *Marie Celeste* out of Kingston and discharged at the West India Docks."

Tom grudgingly stood out of the way and we went down a passageway that had once been limewashed and so into a poorly lit room in which I made out some five figures. In one corner of the room was a bar with a barrel on it and a small selection of bottles on the shelves behind it. This was presided over by a lady whom I should judge was on the wrong side of seventy.

As we entered the room such conversation as there had been diminished and all heads came to look in our direction. The inquisition as to who were were began again, this time from various points in the room.

Naturally I stood silent as Holmes introduced himself as John Clay and me as Abe Slaney. He claimed we had recently docked in the east end of London from a boat that had employed us as deckhands from Jamaica, where we had been left high and dry by another boat being seized by the authorities.

I felt quite embarrassed as Holmes described me as a desperate man, wanted by the police on three continents, the perpetrator of a number of crimes of which murder, kidnapping and obtaining money by menaces seemed the most wholesome. He went on to explain that I had lost my voice after being half-garotted by a Thugee in India, but that I was strong as an ox and twice as willing.

He then lightly sketched in his own biography, which was slightly less reputable than that he had ascribed to me. His crimes included mutiny, bank robbery, kidnap, extortion, grievous bodily harm and safecracking, while his areas of operation included America, the West Indies, Australia, Brazil and Sidcup. He cast himself as a truly villainous figure.

The gang, for there is no other way to corporately describe the group of persons assembled in that dismal room, appeared impressed. One of them volunteered, "Well, if only 'arf of what you say is true, you're the sort of bloke we need."

The man who had been at the door said, "But who says we need anyone else?"

"Since Harry was caught by the Peelers at Chumley's," Ruby informed them, "the Boss says he might need an extra hand."

"But wouldn't he look funny with three hands?" asked the crone behind the bar, who was apparently as stupid as she appeared.

By mutual consent, clearly as a result of past experience, she was ignored by all present. One of them put his finger on what I considered to be a weak link in Holmes' story. "But if you're as all-fired marvellous as you say, how comes it that I 'aven't 'eard about you?"

Holmes riposted with, "Have you been to the West Indies recently?"

The muttered answer was, as expected, in the negative. "Well, there you are then," Holmes was at his most disdainful, "I've done most of my best work there."

Another of them wanted to know if either of us was wanted by the police, to which Holmes replied in the affirmative.

"You'd better get out then," said this worthy, "'cause we don't want no one who is wanted by the rozzers."

"Why not?" asked the doorkeeper of him, "you are, aren't you?"

Ruby interrupted to say that this inquisition was leading nowhere in her opinion and she suggested that the gang's leader be asked if 'John' and 'Abe' should join the group.

"And if he says 'no'," the doorman said, "we know how to deal with 'em." And he drew a finger very suggestively across his own throat, making, as he did so, a nasty gurgling sound.

"We're not worried," claimed Holmes, striking a defiant pose, "let's meet your leader and let him decide."

Ruby smiled, "Now that's the interesting thing about this organisation. We none of us have ever met the Boss. He communicates with us through this - " And she drew back a grubby curtain to reveal, in a recess in the wall, a large horn, such as is used to aid reception from the gramophone, to which were attached a multitude of wires. "John Clay," Ruby said with a flourish of her hand, "meet the Boss!"

The loudspeaker emitted a screech, which moved all the wax round in my ears, and then from it a voice could be heard.

"Welcome, John Clay," said the machine. "I have listened to your conversation and know all about you. So you wish to join us?"

"Yeah," Holmes snarled, "as long as the money's good."

"The money will be very good if you do what

you are told. First of all, may I ask what you know of our little enterprise?"

"Nothing," said Holmes.

"But you will, at least, have heard of our audacious kidnapping of the Princess Fatima from the Hyperion Theatre under the noses of the English police?" queried the voice, which was so distorted that I had great difficulty in understanding what was being said.

"No," replied Holmes unconcernedly.

One of the toughs in the celler interjected, "But you must 'ave. It was all over Town."

"Me and me mate 'ave been at sea, ain't we," Holmes shaped up to him belligerently.

The voice from the horn ignored this little argument. "That job was carried out by us. It was a brilliant piece of work that will bring me in millions. The police are baffled - and will remain so!"

"But how can me and me mate help?" asked Holmes.

"I was quite impressed by your record, I like your style and there are one or two little jobs that I think you could tackle. But before we finally accept you there is a small duty that you must accomplish successfully to prove yourself worthy."

Holmes muttered his grudging agreement to the proposition.

The voice continued, "If you succeed, you will become a full member of my association, if you fail..."

The old lady behind the bar cackled and pointed to a trap that I had not previously noticed by the further wall.

"You'd 'ave a little accident with your throat and you might 'appen to fall through there into the sewers, where the rats 'ud clear up the remains." And the unpleasant old person gave a further explosion of laughter.

"I understand," said Holmes, "it don't worry me and Abe, here, is with me, ain't yer, Abe?"

I nodded vigorously, smiling vacantly the while.

The voice resumed, "For this next operation I require each of you to sign a letter. What the letter contains is of no interest to you whatsoever, but I want each of you to copy the signature on to the piece of paper I have attached."

Ruby called, "Here you are, boys, come over here. Now just copy what's on the bottom of this letter."

One by one the gang laboriously put pen to paper and scratched a quill pen across the letter. Holmes and I were last in the queue and, when it was Holmes' turn, he exclaimed, "This is Sherlock Holmes' monniker, ain't it?"

This remark was ignored, but, when I came to look at the signature, sure enough, it was my friend's own writing. Fearing that my hand might be too cultured for the purpose of forgery, I signed myself with an 'X', which, when the letters were examined by Ruby, drew forth a snort of derision.

The voice on the machine spoke again, "Which is the most accurate?"

Ruby scarcely had to look at the others before proclaiming, "This one. John Clay's."

"Very well," said the voice, "put that one into the cigar box you have and all of you, except Tom and Ruby, get the box delivered at Sherlock Holmes' rooms. I don't care what methods you use, but get it into his possession - without him getting suspicious of you. Do you think you can manage that?"

The assembled company mumbled agreement and we all shuffled off. As we left I heard the voice say to the two remaining, "Ruby. Tom. Now get down to the Hyperion. And, Tom, you know what to do - and who to do it to!"

And so Holmes and I, together with five other shabbily dressed individuals, whose names it emerged were Bob, Jim, Alf, Bert and Alfonso, made our furtive way from Soho to Baker Street, dodging through alleys and mews and keeping as far away from street lights and strolling policemen as possible. I felt very conspicuous and failed to see how the constabulary could not pick us out as being criminals and arrest us all, but I was unable to voice my fears - obviously!

THE PRINCESS

THE PRINCESS

It seemed to take a long time to get to the north end of Baker Street, but get there eventually we did. We stood in a little huddle on the opposite side of the road from 221b and a discussion took place as how best to carry out our mission.

First of all there was great argument about whether this was the Sherlock Holmes' residence or not, which was resolved by Holmes himself going over the road and pointing out to them the highly polished brass shingle 'SHERLOCK HOLMES PRIVATE INVESTIGATOR' that Mrs Hudson had caused to be put by the front door after neighbours had complained of their being pestered by sinister strangers looking for the great man's consulting rooms.

"Now, then," said the individual I had now identified as Bob, "How are we going to get this 'ere box into Sherlock Holmes' place without raising suspicion?"

The man Jim piped up, "I know the answer - and it's simple!"

"It would have to be simple if you had an idea," Bob clearly considered himself to be in charge of the party.

"No," said Jim, "all we got to do is grab this box, take careful aim and chuck it through the winder!"

So saying, he drew back his arm preparatory to lobbing the box upwards. Bob grabbed him.

"If we all stand around here like this," Holmes mildly commented, "someone's going to ask us what we're all doing."

"You're right," agreed Bob. "Now, let's all have a quick think".

"What about," volunteered Alf, "if I was to shin up a drainpipe, force the winder, and slip the box in that way?"

We all contemplated the façade of 221b Baker Street, innocent of any drainpipe. Alf wandered off a little way, kicking a stone.

Alfonso, who had struck me as possibly being a foreigner, now suggested, "If we was to make ourselves into an human pyramid, like my family's circus act, mayhaps the top person like me - could reach the window?"

A bit of argument ensued while it was decided who would be at the base of such a pyramid and Jim and Alf were elected. It was agreed that I should get upon their backs, Bob would climb up me and Alfonso would become the cherry on the cake. Holmes said that he would simply prefer to watch.

Jim and Alf crouched down, but before I could lever myself into position, a patrolling policeman came down the road. Jim and Alf immediately became very interested in the pavement and pretended to be searching for something.

"'Allo, 'allo, 'allo," said the policeman, "Lorst something?"

"Yes, mate," replied Jim, "we're looking for a copper."

The policeman laughed, "Looks like one has found you!" And he strolled off down the street, chuckling to himself at his own wit.

"'Struth," said Bob, mopping his brow, "that was close."

"While that policeman was 'ere, I calculated," said Alfonso, "that the pyramid wouldn't reach, anyway. So that's that!"

"I know," said Jim. "If I cupped my 'ands, like this, and you was to jump into 'em. I could then jerk him upwards and he might reach the windersill."

Rarely have I seen grown men make such spectacles of themselves as did Jim and Alf shortly thereafter. When they picked themselves up, Alf was complaining that he had broken a leg, but this was an exaggeration. How the noise failed to attract a watching crowd I cannot imagine. I was on tenterhooks in case the policeman should return, but luck was with the miscreants.

As they all stood around dusting themselves down, Holmes picked up the box, which had been deposited on the ground, and went towards the front door.

"'Ere!" whispered Bob, "What you doin'?"

Holmes ignored him and knocked on the door. After a short pause it opened and Mrs Hudson was framed in it with the gas light behind her. I could see by the way her eyebrows raised that she recognised Holmes immediately, but she said nothing as my friend put a supplicatory finger to his forehead and whined, "'Scuse me, lady, I was given this to give to Sherlock Holmes. Will you make sure he gets it - it's most important."

"Give it to me," Mrs Hudson took the box, "and now be off with you, you scallywag, you'll get no tip off me."

She slammed the door, leaving a jubilant gang to cluster round Holmes, slapping him on the back and generally congratulating him.

"That was brilliant," claimed Bob. "You're really going to be an asset to us. Let's pop into the Old Mermaid on the way back to celebrate."

It seemed that Holmes and I were now integrated into the gang, an integration that was made even firmer when it was Holmes who put his hand into his pocket when we reached a low ale house in Charlotte Street.

As we merrily turned into the alley where the Den of Thieves was to be found we caught up with Tom, who had been sent to the Hyperion on his mysterious errand, and so we all entered the dive together. The old lady was still behind her counter, seeming not to have budged since we left, while Ruby was lounging on the only comfortable chair.

She got up and moved some kind of switch on the voice machine. "They're all back, Boss," she announced. She then turned back to us and asked how successful we had been.

Bob answered first, boasting of our success at Baker Street. He did have the decency, however, to ascribe the major part of our achievement to 'John Clay', who bowed sardonically to Ruby.

Tom had a fuller tale to tell.

"Like you said, Boss," he started, "I went along to the Hyperion to sort out Marvo. When I got there a lot of them girls was on the stage and that Chairman bloke and Marvo. When I come in the door the bits of skirt done a bit of a scream 'cause I had got me shiv out and was prunin' me fingernails. Well, I soon told 'em I wasn't interested in them - as long as they kept quiet - what I wanted was a quiet chat with Marvo.

"Now Marvo didn't seem too anxious to meet me, so I think that you was right, Boss he's weakening. If the rozzers have another go at him he'll spill the beans and it'll be all up with us. So I thought I'd better sort him out straight away, so I dived after him through the crowd of girls. They all screamed a bit more and got in the way, but I almost put me hands on Marvo, when he jumped into one of his cabinets what was standing by the side of the stage and - vanished.

"I had a good look round, but I couldn't see him anywhere. One of them saucy little donahs said that that was what a magician was supposed to do - do magic. There didn't seem no point in hanging around, so I reminded them all that the big pay out was due in a couple of days' time and come away. If Marvo shows up again - they'll keep him out of harm's way; they want their money - greedy little baggages."

Ruby was not too happy with this speech. "That wasn't too bright, was it, Tom, just leaving Marvo free to go straight to the cops. You were told to eliminate him and you failed. We'll see what the Boss says about that!"

Over the microphone came the voice of the unseen Boss, "It is probably just as well that you didn't make Marvo into cold meat on the stage of the Hyperion. My instructions were for you to silence him by bringing him to the boat - not to kill him then and there. But it probably doesn't matter now, because we are going to wrap up this part of the operation within hours, so even if Marvo does squeal, the law won't be able to touch us - we'll be off and away."

"What about paying the Hyperion people?" asked Ruby.

"They'll have to take their chance. They've served their purpose. If they go to the police they will hardly expect to receive a pension from public funds for their contribution to this little mystery. If they have any sense they'll all stay mum - and that includes Marvo, as well."

91

I could see that Ruby was not too happy about this, but this particular gang of criminals did not seem to have a very high standard of honour amongst themselves. I wondered what promised payment had persuaded a considerable number of the Hyperion staff to join in with this enterprise - although I could still not understand how the actual disappearance had taken place.

"Right now, boys," Ruby clapped her hands together smartly, "we'll all be moving on before long, so you'd better get acquainted with your prize exhibits."

With a theatrical gesture, she drew back a dirty brown curtain that I had not previously observed by the side of the bar. To the applause and catcalls of the gang and the quiet astonishment of myself and, I am sure, Sherlock Holmes, there, sitting bound back to back on a kitchen table were a bearded gentleman and a dark young lady.

Unceremoniously Tom and Jim grabbed them and pulled them off the table, so that they were standing, tied together at the wrists. They were both gagged with very unhygienic looking neckerchieves. As they came into the better, though still atrociously dim, light of the main room, I was astounded to see that the gentleman was none other than the clergyman who had started Holmes off on this escapade, Charles Samuels.

The girl was obviously our quarry. She was slim and barely four feet six inches tall, with a brown complexion, set off by flashing eyes. Her costume was scarcely suitable for English wear and was very incongruous in this present setting. It consisted of gold pointed sandals, a sort of filmy trouser arrangement that revealed more than it covered and a tight corsage in a gold fabric.

Distressed as I was by the sight of this young person in this predicament, I also hoped that the members of the gang were married men, as the Princess' costume allowed more anatomical detail to be observed than is usual outside the matrimonial hearth.

Ruby made a sweeping bow and introduced, "My lords, ladies and gentlemen, may I present the one and only Reverend Charles Samuels and - wait for it, wait for it! - the delectable Princess Fatima!"

The wolf whistles, catcalls and stamping of feet from the assembled gang was ear piercing. How my heart felt for these two respectable people trapped in such a gallery of rogues. Then I remembered that among these rogues were the greatest private investigator in the world and myself, so perhaps things were not as black for the innocent victims of the kidnapping as they might have been.

When their unpleasant display had muted itself, Tom made a mockery of polite etiquette by abasing himself before the Princess and uttering, in a mock-servile tone, "Welcome to our humble abode, Your Princess-ship." Alfonso, not to be outdone, followed this up with, "Please excuse our present quarters - with your help we hope to improve them before too long!"

The rest of the gang thought this highly amusing and fell about laughing. Holmes and I, of course, had to participate in this display of bad manners.

Ruby obviously felt that matters had gone far enough. She addressed herself to Holmes and me. "This, as you have gathered, is our prize, for which we expect to get a Princess's ransom."

"And what will happen to them afterwards," I felt compelled to ask, my humanitarian instincts as a doctor prevailing over good sense, possibly.

"That is not your concern," Ruby informed me icily, "Our Leader has given instructions that there is just one further job to be done to complete this operation. So you will all follow me."

One of the gang asked if he was to bring the two prisoners along, but was told that Old Sal, the aged barmaid, was competent enough to look after them for the few minutes that the rest of us would be absent.

I doubted that Sal was sufficiently capable of looking after herself for any length of time, let alone guard two prisoners who clearly were of prime importance to the criminal activity under progress, but it would ill behove me to point this out.

Led by Ruby the gang filed from the Den of Thieves with Holmes and myself as the last in the line. As we crossed the threshold Holmes stumbled and fell, apparently winding himself as he did so. The others returned and clustered round, but I pushed them to one side while I bent over my friend.

He lay on his back with his eyes tight closed. Through gritted teeth he muttered, "I seem to have turned my ankle. You lot go on without me."

He was obviously in considerable pain, so I indicated in dumb show that I would remain with him, while Ruby led the rest of the gang off wither I knew not.

I assisted Holmes to his feet and, with him leaning heavily on my shoulder, supported him back into the Den of Thieves. I kicked the door shut behind us and, to my surprise, Holmes straightened up and snapped out, "Watson, look after the old lady. I will release these two."

Old Sal behind the bar gave me no trouble as I loosely bound her by the wrists to her own beer pumps. When I had secured her I looked over to Holmes, who was showing no ill effects from his fall, but was teasing open the knots of the thin rope binding Mr Samuels and Princess Fatima together.

94

When they were separated, but still individually cordoned, Homes removed the gag from the Princess' mouth. She immediately reacted by trying to bite Holmes, which he avoided, then she spat copiously at him.

He mopped himself up and mildly remarked, "My dear Princess, I am on your side. We have come to rescue you."

The Princess clearly didn't believe him, despite his actions and words. "Who are you?" she wanted to know.

"My name is Sherlock Holmes and the gentleman standing at the bar is my associate Doctor Watson."

The Princess turned towards me, "Not Doctor Watson, the author?" she enquired.

I blushed with pleasure at being so instantly recognised and shuffled my feet slightly while ackowledging my identity. Meanwhile Holmes ungagged the clergyman, rather roughly, I thought.

Mr Samuels cleared his mouth of the remains of his gag and gasped, "Thank goodness you have come, Mr Holmes, I was beginning to fear for our lives. We have been incarcerated here now for a day and a half without food or drink. I was beginning to lose hope."

I busied myself with untying the last ropes holding Princess Fatima's hands behind her back, while Holmes performed the same office for Mr Samuels. Holmes was quicker than I and, before I had completed my task, the clergyman was shaking Holmes warmly by the hand. I was extremely gratified that, when I finally released the Princess, she threw her arms round my neck and, coquettishly standing on one leg with the other bent backwards at the knee, kissed me soundly on the lips. There are few old codgers rising 50 who can claim to have been so greeted by a 17 year old princess at their first meeting!

When I disentangled myself from the young lady I found Mr Samuels waiting to shake me by the hand - I noticed that the Princess also greeted Sherlock Holmes formally in the same fashion. "It is a pleasure to meet you," said the clergyman, "I've read a lot of your work in the *Strand* magazine."

I may have been imagining, but I could swear that I heard Holmes mutter in the background, "Hasn't everyone?"

"But surely we have met before," I pointed out, "in Baker Street?"

"I regret that I have not had that pleasure," replied Mr Samuels.

"Do you mean to say," I asked, "that the man we met yesterday morning was an imposter?"

"I cannot say, Doctor Watson, but I know that I have been held here by those ruffians since we were abducted on the way to a visit to a music hall two days ago."

While I was mulling this information over Holmes took charge of the situation. "The first thing must be to get this young lady to a place of safety."

Clearly this was the honourable thing to do, so I went towards the door leading to the street. As I was about to open it, it was disconcertingly thrown wide from the other side. In the doorway were Bob, Tom and the other thugs. A couple of them held hand guns at the ready, while all the others carried menacing staves. I drew back.

"Come in, gentlemen," said Mr Samuels, "allow me to introduce to you the great detective, Sherlock Holmes, and his biographer, John Watson."

Before anyone else could intervene Holmes turned, grasped Mr Samuels' great bushy beard and pulled. I winced at the pain that this exercise must be causing, when with a ripping sound, the beard came away in Holmes' hands.

"In my turn," and Holmes bowed perfunctorily in my direction, "allow me to introduce Colonel James Moriarty, elder brother of the arch criminal, Professor Moriarty."

I was aware that my mouth had dropped open.

"And," Holmes continued, "I don't know this young lady's name, but I can state confidently that she has probably not been nearer to the Persian Gulf than Brighton."

By now I was completely dumbfounded.

"Go on, Mr Holmes," invited the erstwhile Mr Samuels, busily engaged in picking odd straggles of beard from his face.

"I had my suspicions about you, Colonel," said Holmes, "when you first visited us in Baker Street."

"But," I interjected, "he said he hadn't called on us."

"I regret, Watson, that not everything that the reverend gentleman has told us, either then or more recently, bears the stamp of complete veracity. When he visited us in Baker Street, I repeat, I wondered at certain Americanisms in his vocabulary not usual in an English clergyman, although these could have been dismissed because of his wider overseas experience, but I was convinced that his beard was false when I detected a smell of bay rum - patted on the face **after** shaving - and of gum arabic - used to afix an imitation hirsute appendage to his clean-shaven cheeks. If the beard was false, I reasoned, the story that he told was very likely false as well."

It has been my privilege to see many wrong doers confronted by Holmes' logic and the reaction is very often the same. "Very clever, Mr Holmes," sneered Moriarty, "but, tell me, what reasoning led you to this place and into my clutches?"

"My reference collection of books and newspaper cuttings revealed no Samuels as a missionary in the Persian Gulf area, but I cannot claim to have records of all King Edward's subjects. However, they did tell me that a petty king from that area, named Aziz, did have a daughter Fatima. but she is only nine years old. Any other Aziz Fatima connections failed to come to light, so I concluded that the entire entourage was suspect. Having been implicated by suggestion through a piece of headgear and then being approached by yourself in disguise, intrigued me sufficiently to try to find out what lay behind this sham. And so you find me here. But, pray inform me, what does lie behind this charade?"

"You killed my brother at the Reichenbach Falls," snarled our captor, for, by this time, we had been seized by the gang and were being restrained with our arms painfully locked behind us. "I swore then to get my revenge on Sherlock Holmes."

"Revenge is a debilitating pastime," Holmes observed mildly, "this whole enterprise has clearly taken a considerable amount of time and money. Why does a talented man like you allow himself to be controlled by an obsession? Your brother's death, though regretable, was richly deserved and the account should be closed."

"The sheer pleasure of watching a man of your ability fall for my little plan, allowing yourself to become, I might express it, the cheese in the mousetrap, has made it all worthwhile. Thank you, Mr Holmes."

While all attention was focussed on Holmes and Moriarty I took the opportunity to try to break free. I threw off the hands of Tom and Alfonso and made a dash for the door, but was felled by a blow in the midriff from a warming pan wielded by Old Sal, who seemed to bear me some malice for having tied her up.

As I lay gasping on the floor, the door opened and a female entered. From my situation I could not see her face, but Moriarty introduced her. "Mr Holmes, I would like you to meet Miss Lily Nightingale, the chanteuse. But, of course, you have already met, haven't you?"

Holmes ignored the girl, who stood indecisively by, and spoke directly to Moriarty. "How did you make her work for you?"

"If she doesn't do as she is told I can give the police evidence to implicate her brother in a particularly nasty murder and he will certainly hang. Isn't that so, my dear?"

By now I had been dragged to my feet and I could see Lily reluctantly nod her head.

Moriarty, in complete control of everyone present either by physical or moral force, gloated further. "I find it entertaining that a man with a reputed dislike of womankind should be trapped by two of them. You see, Mr Holmes, when I heard that you had run away from the police I guessed that you would attempt to infiltrate my humble organisation, so, despite your disguise, we knew it was you from the moment you entered these portals. Amusing, isn't it?"

"About as funny, Moriarty," replied Holmes, "as that snake you arranged to have left in my rooms."

"Yes," agreed Moriarty, "Lily was very helful about that. I thought it might further provoke your interest."

"And the egg?" pursued Holmes.

"What egg?" asked Moriarty. Behind him I could see Lily Nightingale imperceptibly shaking her head.

Holmes caught her eye and changed the subject. "What are your further plans now, Colonel?"

"That will have to wait until later tonight. In the meantime, perhaps you would care to tell me how you deduced yourself into this situation? How, for example, do you think the disappearance of the Princess was arranged at the Hyperion?"

"Oh, that," said Holmes dismissively, "that was elementary. When Marvo called for a volunteer from the audience this young lady - who is she, by the way?..."

"She's my kid sister, if you really want to know," said Ruby, speaking for the first time since the re-arrival of the gang.

"...this young lady jumped up. Once on stage as she is of petite stature she was given a box to stand upon. She was then covered with a sheet and the fake jewels were placed upon the dummy. Obviously a number of the music hall performers were involved as, when the jewels burst into flame and the attention of the audience was distracted, this young person, clearly a skilled contortionist trained possibly by her sister, folded herself into an impossibly small space inside the box and - er - disappeared. In the ensuing commotion it was easy for the box to be dragged off stage, when this girl extracted herself, removed her skin colouring make-up and rather distinctive costume and slipped off. It was purely by chance that Doctor Watson discovered the box and that I noticed a trace of grease paint on the lid. The traditional magician's ploy of misdirection had been used brilliantly."

"Excellent, Mr Holmes," Moriarty congratulated my friend. "What a pity it is that this will be your very last deduction."

Ruby and her sister were talking in a corner and I realised that, during the preceeding conversation, Lily Nightingale had slipped from the room, unnoticed - certainly by me and, I think, by anyone else.

100

"What a pity it is," mused Moriarty, "that the greatest brain in Christendom will soon be stilled."

Holmes, defiant even when the odds are stacked against him, said, "You cannot have met my brother, Mycroft!"

I had earlier deduced that this Colonel Moriarty was not quite balanced and this chance remark seemed to tip him over an edge. "Enough of this buffoonery," he screamed. "Deal with them!"

And I received a heavy blow from one of my captors across the back of my neck. For a second, as my eyelids closed, I saw every hue of the colour red, then total darkness overwhelmed me.

THE DOCK

THE DOCK

Dimly I recall being bundled into a cart and trundled through many a cobbled passage. How I retained any senses at all I cannot say, but it was lucky that I did for I was able to 'play possum' - as our American cousins say - when I was unceremoniously dumped on to a wooden floor and slapped around the face. Not by so much as a flicker of an eyelid did I reveal that I had partially regained consciousness and I was left where I fell, the ruffians assuming that I posed no threat.

I stole my eyelids open a fraction to see what was going on and found myself on the stage of the Hyperion Music Hall!

The last performance of the evening - not including, I imagine, the Great Marvo - had finished long since and there was only left on stage what the theatrical profession call a 'worker light'. This cast strange shadows, but as I accustomed myself to them I was able to see, without moving myself in any way, Moriarty ranging round the stage, like a lion in a cage. Were I his doctor I would recommend that he seek the advice of an alienist forthwith.

In mid-stage there was a table and on it, with his face looking straight upwards into the dark flies of the theatre, was my friend, still unconscious, as far as I could judge from my undignified position.

As I watched, Jim and Alfonso finished tying Holmes to the table in a very rough and ready, although effective, manner. I braced myself for my turn, but, to my astonishment, they seemed to have forgotten me! I continued observing the scene until such time as I could make an effective contribution.

Moriarty dismissed his men with a foul oath and dashed a glass of water on to Holmes' face. My friend groaned and opened his eyes. He attempted to bring a hand to his head, but was prevented by his bonds. It may be a literary cliché, but I have to record that Holmes then groaned, "Where am I?"

Moriarty chortled his glee, "You, my fine feathered friend, are on the stage of the Hyperion Theatre, where the mystery started and where, for you, it will all end." He then erupted into a whole series of hysterical laughs that made me doubt his stability.

Holmes, sensing that the only way he might manage to free himself was to engage this maniac in speech, then asked, "What are you going to do with me?"

After a further explosion of laughter, Moriarty giggled, "Now that's the clever part! As you might be able to see there is a large sandbag hanging in the flies straight over your head. Now when I set this timing device" - and Moriarty gestured to a part of the stage that was obscured from my sight - "you have just three minutes to live. When the dial reaches zero it will release a cord and the bag will fall smashing your head to pulp."

"But what is the point?" Holmes asked in a very reasonable tone of voice. "Why not simply shoot me and have done with it?"

"That wouldn't suit my plan at all, Mr Holmes. You destroyed my brother and now I

106

propose to more than just kill you. I am going to destroy your reputation. It will be rumoured around that the kidnap was your plan to win yourself a little nest egg for your retirement and that when it went disastrously wrong, you disposed of your victims and then killed yourself with a characteristically ingenious method of suicide."

Holmes gave a short laugh. "No one will ever believe scandal of that sort."

"Mud sticks, Mr Holmes, especially when it is backed up with the facts of your running from the police and the confession note that you so kindly signed - and delivered!" Moriarty again threw back his head to give out a laugh the like of which I hope never to hear again.

Sherlock Holmes appeared to be losing his ice cold nerve. "You'll never get away with this," he said.

"But it looks as if I have," returned Colonel Moriarty. "From now" - and he fiddled with something just out of my vision - "you have just about three minutes to live. It will be pleasant to think of you praying that my mechanism will not function. I wonder if all your past cases will flash before your mind's eye as the seconds tick away."

Ruby and one of the men - I could not distinguish which in the gloom - came in from one of the wings and Ruby whispered that the boat was ready.

"Very good, my dear," said Moriarty, "now you go and join your music hall colleagues, while Bob and I -"

Ruby interrupted, "But I want to go with you. I want to get what's mine from this job."

"Don't worry, my dear, you'll get everything that's coming to you," leered the Colonel. He then turned formally to Holmes, inclined his head, clicked his heels and said, "Pray excuse me, Mr Holmes, but

I have an appointment with a watery saint. I send you my deceased brother's compliments."

And all three quickly left the stage.

Immediately I struggled to my feet, thankful that I had been forgotten in the general excitement. I found that one of my legs had gone to sleep and I suffered excruciating pins and needles, which seemed to adversely affect the wound I received years ago in Afghanistan.

I staggered over to Holmes and asked him how he felt.

His reply was brusque, I felt, and with no words of welcome, "Stop that timer, Watson!"

I limped over to the mechanism which, I now saw, resembled nothing so much as a metronome as used by the more pedantic of our orchestral conductors and players. I bent to examine this, but was frustrated by a sort of locking device that seemed immovable. Nevertheless I wrestled with it for a few seconds, while Holmes got increasingly agitated in his speech.

When I get flustered my reactions tend to slow down, so I dithered with the metronome for longer than I should perhaps. I was halted in my efforts by Holmes bellowing, "Move the table, Watson!"

For a few precious seconds I failed to comprehend what Holmes was talking about, then I realised the situation and gave the table a push up stage. It was just as well that I stepped back from doing that as immediately the sandbag in the flies dropped on to the stage where I had been standing after moving the table and burst, scattering gravel all over the place.

I mopped my brow with a shaky hand. I had come very near death. And so, of course, had my friend, who, it came to me, was still tied to the table. I went over to him and asked him how he felt.

His reply was still unfriendly in the circumstances, "Damn it, get me out of this, Watson."

Had I been in Holmes' place, I hope that I would have expressed pleasure at seeing an old friend again, particularly one who has pushed you out of the way of a falling sandbag, but that is not Holmes' way.

By my attitude I demonstrated, I believe, that my feelings were hurt, but I nevertheless undid the ropes binding Holmes to the table. When he was free, he sat up and began massaging his legs.

"Moriarty is only a few minutes ahead of us. He said that he was on his way to a watery saint and we know that he has a boat ready. The only watery saint I can immediately recall in London is St Katherine. Her docks are down by the Tower, so we might be able to catch him. Come along, Watson."

I protested that we should invoke the assistance of the Metropolitan Police, but Holmes said there was no time and so we dashed out of the Stage Door of the Hyperion into Surrey Street, where by singular chance a cab was passing. We bundled into it, Holmes shouting to the driver to get us to East Smithfield as quickly as possible.

The driver responded gallantly to the challenge - as did his horse - and we rattled busily down Fleet Street and up Ludgate Hill to pass St Paul's Cathedral at a gallop. Our pace slackened slightly in Cannon Street on the long pull up to the junction with London Bridge and then picked up again down Eastcheap and Byward Street. We bowled merrily past Tower Hill and the Tower of London, where so much English History has been witnessed, and drew up, the horse well lathered, just past the Royal Mint.

Holmes threw the cabby a couple of

sovereigns - a justifiable extravagence in the circumstances - and we ran into the purlieus of St Katherine's Dock. Once inside, Holmes waved me to stay back and he slipped cautiously from shadow to shadow, beckoning me on as he discovered the way ahead was safe.

We had progressed in this fashion for about two hundred yards, when Holmes motioned for me to take care to be quiet. I crept up to his position behind a stack of barrels and peered tentatively round the edge.

We had caught up with Moriarty and Ruby! They were just arriving and were greeting the others in the gang. I heard Moriarty say, "Gentlemen, everything seems to be proceeding according to plan. The police should be discovering Holmes' body in about an hour from now, by which time we will be long gone."

One of the roughs said that 'the girl', by which I imagined that he meant Ruby's young sister, was on board and asked what was to be done with her.

"She has outlived her usefulness to us, I regret to say," Moriarty was without scruples. "Her body will be found floating in the Thames tomorrow, I should think."

Ruby's reaction to this was quite natural in that she threw herself at Moriarty, attempting to scratch his eyes out. He felled her with a single blow and drew back his leg preparatory to kicking her where she lay, but before he could demonstrate how little of a gentleman he was Holmes stepped into the light cast by the gang's torches.

"Not so fast, Colonel Moriarty," he snapped.

If Moriarty was startled to see Holmes still in the land of the living he did not show it by the movement of a single muscle. "Mr Holmes," he greeted, "I really must congratulate you on your

110

powers of survival, but you're too late. As you can see, you are outnumbered."

The gang surged towards Holmes and me, but Holmes stopped them with a pre-emptory gesture. "As I thought, you have to hide behind hired help," he haughtily remarked.

"So you want a man to man fight, Marquis of Queensbury rules, do you, Mr Holmes? I'm always ready to oblige." Moriarty spoke to his men with dignity. "You lot, get on the barge, I will join you in just a moment."

The gang shuffled off, dragging Ruby's still unconscious body with them.

"So," said Holmes, "face to face on equal terms. Put them up!" And Holmes struck a conventional pugilistic pose.

Colonel James Moriarty simply sneered at Holmes, "Do you think I would brawl like a common ruffian? You beat my brother in a scuffle, but this time I have the advantage!"

And so saying, he produced a revolver and levelled it at Sherlock Holmes. He had cocked the firing piece, when there was a commotion a little way off. As his attention was distracted Holmes dived for Moriarty's legs in a rugby tackle and they landed on the quayside with limbs entangled.

Before I had taken breath to join in this fracas Inspector Lestrade and a handful of his men came into view and challenged Moriarty to submit.

This distracted Holmes' attention from the matter in hand and Moriarty, with an agility surprising in a man who must have been in his late forties, slipped from Holmes' grasp and bounded on to a flat headed bollard, from whence he menaced Lestrade and the policemen.

Holmes, winded on the ground, warned that the gun was loaded, but Lestrade, in the best traditions of Scotland Yard, did not hesitate. He

111

walked deliberately towards Moriarty saying, "Put that gun down, laddie, you'll only make it worse for yourself. You can't get away. The place is surrounded."

Moriarty scoffed. "I think not. He who fights and runs away, lives to fight another day. Eh, Sherlock?" And, in a single movement he threw his gun into Lestrade's face and half-turning, dived into the dark waters of the dock.

We all rushed to the edge of the quay, but the blackness of the night and the water had quite swallowed Colonel James Moriarty. It was useless to stare into nothing, so we turned away.

"He is finished with," Lestrade said, as he shook Holmes' hand in greeting.

"I wonder. The Moriarty's are a long lived race. You will recall, Lestrade, that the late Professor also had a younger brother, somehow connected with the railways of Somerset. It might be as well to check down in the West Country to see if our recent acquaintance shows up down there."

Lestrade was not to be put down. "At least that is another case satisfactorily completed."

I felt compelled to say that it might not have been so satisfactory had Lestrade and his colleagues not turned up at the crucial moment. How, I wondered, had this fortuitous arrival happened?

"This young lady came to Scotland Yard," said Lestrade, "and convinced me that evil doings were afoot."

He held his hand out in greeting and forward stepped Lily Nightingale!

Sherlock Holmes bowed over her hand and kissed it. "We owe you a very great debt," he said.

Lily coloured prettily. "I couldn't let anything happen to the greatest detective in the world as a result of my wrong-doing," she said.

The rest is history.

The police rounded up the remainder of the gang on the barge and certain charges were made against them and some members of the Hyperion cast. I was pleased that justice was merciful and all the sentences were comparitively light.

Miss Lily Nightingale has pursued her career with modest success and Holmes and I regularly receive invitations to many of the Number Ones - as the top flight of music halls are called.

Of Colonel James Moriarty there has been no further word, but whether he perished in the waters of St Katherine's Dock or if he escaped to continue harbouring revenge against Sherlock Holmes, who can tell?

Holmes' name was, of course, exonerated from any suggestion of a connection with the disappearance of 'Princess Fatima' and he was soon involved in investigations that I have previously chronicled, like 'Shoscombe Old Place' and 'The Three Garridebs'.

On the 26 June I opened my practice in Queen Anne Street, employing as my receptionist a retired music hall artiste named Miss Tilly Footage, a constant reminder of the excitements of the Baker Street exploit that I have called
'Sherlock Holmes
and the Arabian Princess'

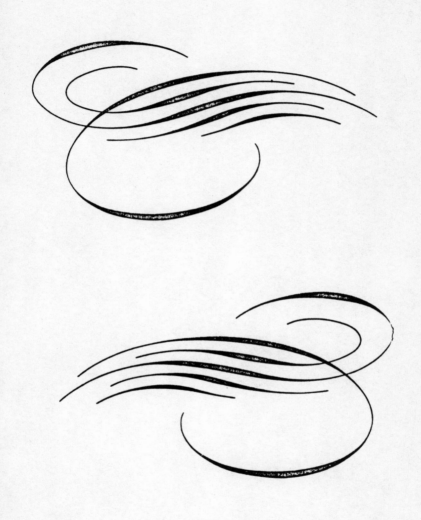